KEITH LAUMER

IT'S A MAD, MAD, MAD GALAXY

A BERKLEY MEDALLION BOOK
PUBLISHED BY
BERKLEY PUBLISHING CORPORATION

Published by arrangement with
the author's agent

ACKNOWLEDGMENTS

"The Body Builders," copyright © 1966 by Galaxy
Publishing Corporation

"The Planet Wreckers," copyright © 1966 by
Galaxy Publishing Corporation

"The War with the Yukks," copyright © 1965
Galaxy Publishing Corporation

"The Star-Sent Knaves," copyright © 1963
Galaxy Publishing Corporation

BERKLEY MEDALLION EDITION, DECEMBER, 1968

BERKLEY MEDALLION BOOKS are published by
Berkley Publishing Corporation
200 Madison Avenue
New York, N.Y. 10016

BERKLEY MEDALLION BOOKS ® TM 757,375

Printed in the United States of America

TABLE OF CONTENTS

THE BODY BUILDERS

He was a big bruiser in a Gendye Mark Seven Sullivan, the luxury model with the nine-point sensory system, the highest-priced Grin-U-Matic facial expression attachment on the market and genuine human hair, mustache and all.

He came through the dining room entry like Genghis Kahn invading a Swiss convent. If there'd been a door in his way he'd have kicked it down. The two lads walking behind him—an old but tough-looking utility model of Liston and a fairly new Wayne—kept their hands in their pockets and flicked their eyes over the room like buggy whips. The head waiter popped out with a stock of big purple menus, but the Sullivan went right past him, headed across toward my table like a field marshal leading a victory parade.

Lorena was with me that night, looking classy in a flossed-up Dietrich that must have set her back a month's salary. She was in her usual mood for the usual reason: she wanted to give up her job at the Cent-Prog and sign a five-year marriage contract with me. The idea left me cold as an Eskimo's tombstone. In the first place, at the rate she burned creds, I'd have to creak around in a second-hand Lionel with about thirty percent sensory coverage and an undersized power core; and in the second, I was still carrying the torch for Julie. Sure, Julie had nutty ideas about Servos. According to her, having a nice wardrobe of specialized outfits for all occasions was one step below cannibalism.

"You and that closet full of zombies!" she used to shake her finger under my nose. "How could a girl possibly marry you and never know what face she'd see when she woke up in the morning!"

She was exaggerating, but that was the way those Organo-Republicans are. No logic in 'em. After all, doesn't it make sense to keep your organic body on file in the Municipal Vaults, safe out of the weather, and let a comfortable, late-model Servo do your walking and talking? Our grandparents found out it was a lot safer and easier to sit in front of the TV screen with feely and smelly attachments than to be out bumping heads with a crowd. It wasn't long after that that they developed the contact screens to fit your eyeballs, and the plug-in audio, so you began to get the real feel of audience participation. Then, with the big improvements in miniaturization and the new tight-channel transmitters, you could have your own private man-on-the-street pickup. It could roam, seeing the sights, while you racked out on the sofa.

Of course, with folks spending so much time flat on their backs, the Public Health boys had to come up with gear to keep the organic body in shape. For a while, people made it with part-time exercise and home model massage and feeding racks, but it wasn't long before they set up the Central File system.

Heck, the government already had everything about you on file, from your birth certificate to your fingerprints. Why not go the whole hog and file the body too?

Of course, nobody had expected what would happen when the quality of the sensory pickups and playbacks got as good as they did. I mean the bit the eggheads call "personality gestalt transfer." But it figured. A guy always had the feeling that his consciousness was sitting somewhere back of his eyes; so when the lids were linked by direct hookup to the Servo, and all the other senses tied in—all of a sudden, you were *there*. The brain was back in Files, doped to the hairline, but you—the thing you call a mind—was there, inside the Servo, living it up.

And with that kind of identification, the old type utilitarian models went out of style, fast. People wanted Servos that expressed the real inner man—the guy you should have been. With everybody as big and tough as they wanted to be, depending on the down payment they could handle, nobody wanted to take any guff off

6

anybody. In the old days, a fellow had to settle for a little fender-bending; now you could hang one on the other guy, direct. Law Cent had to set up a code to cover the problem, and now when some bird insulted you or crowded you off the Fastwalk, you slugged it out with a Monitor watching.

Julie claimed it was all a bunch of nonsense; that the two Servos pounding each other didn't prove anything. She could never see that with perfect linkage, you *were* the Servo. Like now: The waiter had just put a plate of *consomme au beurre blanc* in front of me, and with my high-priced Yum-gum palate accessory, I'd get the same high-class taste thrills as if the soup was being shoved down my Org's mouth in person. It was a special mixture, naturally, that lubricated my main swivel and supplied some chemicals to my glandular analogs. But the flavor was there.

And meanwhile, the old body was doing swell on a nutrient-drip into the femoral artery. So it's a little artificial maybe—but what about the Orggies, riding around in custom-built cars that are nothing but substitute personalities, wearing padded shoulders, contact lenses, hearing aides, false teeth, cosmetics, elevator shoes, rugs to cover their bald domes. If you're going to wear false eyelashes, why not false eyes? Instead of a nose bob, why not bob the whole face? At least a fellow wearing a Servo is honest about it, which is more than you can say for an Orggie doll in a foam-rubber bra—not that Julie needed any help in that department.

I dipped my big silver spoon in and had the first sip just under my nose when the Sullivan slammed my arm with his hip going past. I got the soup square in the right eye. While I was still clicking the eyelid, trying to clear the lens, the Liston jarred my shoulder hard enough to rattle my master solenoid.

Normally, I'm a pretty even-tempered guy. it's my theory that the way to keep a neurotronic system in shape is to hold the glandular inputs to a minimum. But, what with the big event coming up that night, and Lorena riding me hard on the joys of contract life, I'd had a hard day. I hopped up, overrode the eye-blink reflex, made a long

7

reach and hooked a finger in the Liston's collar going away.

"Hold it right there, stumblebum!" I gave the collar a flick to spin him around.

He didn't spin. Instead, my elbow joint made a noise like a roller skate hitting loose gravel; the jerk almost flipped me right on my face.

The Liston did a slow turn, like a ten-ton crane rig, looked me over with a pair of yellow eyes that were as friendly as gun barrels. A low rumbling sound came out of him. I was a little shook but mad enough not to let it bother me.

"Let's have that license number," I barked at him. "There'll be a bill for the eye and another one for a chassis checkup!"

The Wayne had turned, too, and was beetling his brows at me. The big shot Sullivan pushed between the two of them, looked me over like I was something he'd found curled up in a doorway.

"Maybe you better kind of do a fade, Jasper," he boomed loud enough for everybody in the restaurant to hear. "My boys got no sense of humor."

I had my mouth open for my next mistake when Lorena beat me to it:

"Tell the big boob to get lost, Barney; he's interrupting what I was saying to you."

The Sullivan rolled an eye at her, showing off his independent suspension. "Shut your yap, sister," he said.

That did it. I slid my left foot forward, led with a straight left to the power pack, then uppercut him with everything I was able to muster.

My right arm went dead to the shoulder. The Sullivan was still standing there, looking at me. I was staring down at my own fist, dangling at my side. Then it dawned on me what was wrong.

For the moment, I'd forgotten I was wearing a light sport-model body.

2

Gully Fishbein, my business manager, Servo-therapist, drinking buddy, arena trainer and substitute old-maid aunt had warned me I might pull a stunt like this some day. He was a Single-Servo Socialist himself, and in addition to his political convictions, he'd put a lot of time and effort into building me up as the fastest man with a net and mace in show business. He had an investment to protect.

"I'm warning you, Barney," he used to shove an untrimmed hangnail under my nose and yell. "One day you're gonna get your reflexes crossed and miss your step on the Fastwalk—or gauge a close one like you was wearing your Astaire and bust the neck of that Carnera you wasted all that jack on. And then where'll you be, hah?"

"So I lose a hulk," I'd come back. "So what? I've got a closet full of spares."

"Yeah? And what if it's a total? You ever heard what can happen to your mind when the connection's busted—and I do mean busted—like that?"

"I wake up back in my Org body; so what?"

"Maybe," Gully would shake his head and look like a guy with dangerous secrets. "And maybe not . . ."

While I was thinking all this, the Sullivan was getting his money's worth out of the Grin-U-Matic. He nodded and rocked back on his heels, taking his time with me. The talk had died out at the tables around us. Everybody was catching an ear full.

"A wisey," the Sullivan says, loud. "What's the matter, Cheapie, tired of life outside a repair depot?"

"What do you mean, 'Cheapie'?" I said, just to give my Adam's apple a workout. "This Arcaro cost me plenty . . . and this goon of yours has jarred my contacts out of line. Just spring for a checkup and I'll agree to forget the whole thing."

"Yeah." He was still showing me the expensive grin. "I'll bet you will, pint-size." He cocked an eye at the Wayne. "Now, let's see, Nixie, under the traffic code, I got a couple courses of action, right?"

"Cream duh pansy and let's shake a ankle, Boss. I'm hungry." Nixie folded a fist like a forty-pound stake mallet and moved in to demonstrate his idea.

"Nah." The Sullivan stopped him with the back of his hand against his starched shirt front. "The guy pops me first, right? He wants action. So I give him action. Booney." He snapped his fingers and the Liston thumbed a shirt stud.

"For the record," the Sullivan said in a businesslike voice. "Notice of Demand for Satisfaction, with provocation, under Section 991-b, Granyauck 6-78." I heard the whir and click as the recorder built into the Liston's thorax took it down and transmitted it to Law Central.

All of a sudden my mouth was dry.

Sometimes those Servo designers got a little *too* realistic. I tapped a switch in my lower right premolar to cut out the panic-reaction circuit. I'd been all set for a clip on the jaw, an event that wouldn't be too good for the Arcaro, but nothing a little claim to Law Cent wouldn't fix up. But now it was dawning like sunrise over Mandalay that Big Boy had eased me into a spot—or that I'd jumped into it, mouth first. *I'd hit him.* And the fact that he'd put my consomme in my eye first wouldn't count—not to Law Cent. He had the right to call me out—a full-scale Servo-to-Servo match—and the choice of weapons, ground, time, everything was his.

"Tell the manager to clear floor number three," the Sullivan rapped out to the Wayne. "My favorite ground." He winked at Lorena. "Nine kills there, baby. My lucky spot."

"Whatever you say," I felt myself talking too fast. "I'll be back here in an hour, raring to go."

"Nix, Cheapie. The time is now. Come as you are; I ain't formal."

"Why, you can't do that," Lorena announced. Her voice tapes were off key, I noticed; she had a kind of shrill, whiney tone. "Barney's only wearing that little old Arcaro!"

"See me after, doll," the Sullivan cut her off. "I like your style." He jerked his head at the Wayne. "I'll take

10

this clown bare-knuck, Mixie, Naples rules." He turned away, flexing the oversized arms that were an optional extra with the late-model Gendyes. Lorena popped to her feet, gave me the dirtiest look the Dietrich could handle.

"You and that crummy Arcaro." She stuck it in me like a knife. "I wanted you to get a Flynn, with the—"

"Spare me the technical specs, kid," I growled. I was getting the full picture of what I'd been suckered into. The caper with the soup hadn't been any accident. The timing was perfect; I had an idea the Liston was wired a lot better than he looked. Somebody with heavy credits riding on that night's bout was behind it; somebody with enough at stake to buy all the muscle-Servos he needed to pound me into a set of loose nerve ends waving around like worms in a bait can. Busting the Arcaro into a pile of scrap metal and plastic wouldn't hurt my Org physically—but the trauma to my personality, riding the Servo, would be for real. It took steel nerve, cast-iron confideice, razor-edge reflexes and a solid killer's instinct to survive in the arena. After all, anybody could lay out for a Gargantua Servo, if that was all it took; the timing, and pace, and ringcraft that made me a winner couldn't survive having a body pounded to rubble around me. I'd be lucky if I ever recovered enough to hold a coffee cup one-handed.

The Floor Manager arrived, looking indignant; nobody had called him to okay the fracas. He looked at me, started to wave me off, then did a double take.

"*This* is the aggressor party?" The eyebrows on his Menjou crawled up into his hairline.

"That's right," I give it to him fast and snappy. "The bum insulted my lady-friend. Besides which, I don't like his soup-strainer. After I break his rib cage down to chopsticks, I'm going to cut half of it off and give it to the pup to play with." After all, if I was going to get pulverized, I might as well do it in style.

The Sullivan growled.

"You can talk better than that." I pushed up close to him; my nose was on a level with the diamond stickpin in his paisley foulard. "What's your name, Big Stuff? Let's have that registration."

"None of your pidgin, Wisey." He had a finger all ready

11

to poke at me, saw the Monitor coming up ready to quote rules, used it to scratch his ear instead. The big square fingernail shredded plastic off the lobe; he was a little more nervous than he acted. That cinched it: he knew who I was—Barney Ramm, light-heavy champ in the armed singles.

"Assembly and serial numbers, please," the Monitor said. He sounded a little impatient. I could see why he might. It was customary for a challenger to give me the plate data without being asked—especially a floor-vet like Sullivan. He was giving the official a dirty look.

"Where's Slickey?" he growled.

"He doesn't come on for another fifteen minutes," the Monitor snapped. "Look here——"

"*You* look here, Short-timer," the Sullivan grunted. The Wayne moved up to help him give the fellow the cold eye. He glared back at them—for about two seconds. Then he wilted. The message had gotten through. The fix was in.

"Where's the men's room?" I piped up, trying to sound as friskey as ever, but at the moment my mind felt as easy to read as a ninety-foot glare-sign.

"Eh?" The Monitor cut his eyes at me, back at the Sullivan, back to me, like a badminton fan at a championship match. "No," he said. He pushed out his lips and shook his head. "I'm ruling——"

"Rule my foot." I jostled him going past. "I know my rights." I kept going, marched across the dance floor to the discreet door back of the phony palm tree. Inside, I went into high gear. There was a row of coin-operated buffing and circuit-checking machines down one wall, a power core dispenser, a plug-in recharge unit, a nice rack of touch-up paints, a big bin of burned-out reflex coils, and a dispenser full of replacement gaskets with a sign reading FOR SAFETY'S SAKE—PREVENTS HOT BEARINGS.

I skidded past them, dived through an archway into the service area. There were half a dozen padded racks here, loops of power leads, festoons of lube conduit leading down from ceiling-mounted manifolds. A parts index covered the far wall. There was no back door.

"Kindly take (click) position numbered one," a canned voice cackled at me. "Use the console provided to indicate required services. Say, fellow, may I recommend this week's special, Slideeze, the underarm lubricant with a diff——"

I slapped the control plate to shut the pitch off. Coming in here suddenly didn't seem as cute as it had ten seconds earlier. I was cornered—and an accident on a lube-rack would save any possible slip-up on the floor. A little voice about as subtle as a jack-hammer was yelling in my ear that I had half a minute, if I was lucky, before a pair of heavies came through the door to check me out . . . .

It was three quick steps to the little stub wall that protected the customers from the public eye. I flattened myself against the wall beside it just as big feet clumped outside. The door banged open. The Wayne wasn't bothering about being subtle. I wasn't either. I hooked his left instep, spun in behind him, palmed his back hard. He hit face-first with a slam like two garbage flats colliding, and started looping the loop on the tiled floor. Those Waynes always did have a glass jaw. I didn't stick around to see if anybody heard him pile in; I jumped him, slid out through the door. The Liston was standing on the other side of the palm, not ten feet away. I faded to the right, saw another door. The glare sign above it said LADIES. I thought it over for about as long as it takes a clock to say "tick" and dived through.

3

Even under the circumstances it was kind of a shock to find myself standing there staring at pink and turquoise service racks, gold-plated perfume dispensers, and a big display rack full of strictly feminine spares that were enough to make a horse blush.

Then I saw *her*. She was a neat-looking Pickford—the traditional models were big just then. She had fluffy blonde hair, and her chassis covers were off to the waist. I gaped at her, sitting there in front of the mirror, then gulped like a seal swallowing a five-pound salmon. She jumped and swiveled my way, and I got a load of big blue

13

eyes and a rosebud mouth that was opening up to scream.

"Don't yell, lady!" I averted my eyes—an effort like uprooting saplings. "The mob's after me. Just tell me how to get out of here!"

I heard feet outside. So did she, I guess.

"You—you can go out through the delivery door," a nice little voice said. I flicked an eye her way. She was holding a lacy little something over her chest. It slipped when she pointed and I got an eyeful of some of the nicest moulded foam-plastic you'd care to see.

"Thanks, baby, you're a doll," I choked out and went past her, not without a few regrets. The door she'd showed me was around a corner at the back. There was a big carton full of refills for the cosmetics vendor beside it, with the top open. On impulse, I reached in and grabbed one going past.

The door opened into an alley about four feet wide, with a single-rail robo-track down the center for service and delivery mechs. The wall opposite was plain duralith; it went up, a sheer rise without a foothold for a gnat. In both directions the alley was a straight shot for fifty feet to a rectangle of hard late-afternoon sunlight. I could take my choice.

Something clattered to the right. I saw a small custodial cart move jerkily out of a doorway, swing my way, picking up speed. I started to back away; the thing was heavy enough to flatten my Arcaro without slowing down. Then a red light blinked on the front of the thing. It made screechy noises and skidded to a stop.

"Kindly clear the rail," a fruity voice hooted. "This is your busy Sani-mat Service Unit, bringing that Sani-mat sparkle to another satisfied customer!"

A kind of idea formed up somewhere under my hairpiece. I eased around to the side of the machine, a tight squeeze. It was a squatty, boxy job, with a bunch of cleaning attachments racked in front and a good-sized bin behind, half full of what it had been collecting. I got the lip up, climbed up as it started forward again, and settled down in the cargo. It was lumpy and wet, and you could have hammered the aroma out into horseshoes. I guess the

14

world has made a lot of progress in the last few decades, but garbage still smells like garbage.

I estimated I'd covered a hundred feet or less, when the cart braked to a sudden stop. I heard voices; something clicked and a hum started up near my left ear.

"Kindly clear the rail," the take said. "This is your Sanirat Service Uuwwrrr——"

The cart jumped and I got another faceful of garbage. Somebody—it sounded like the Wayne—yelled something. I got set, ready to come out swinging as soon as the lid went up. But the voices faded out, and I heard running feet. The cart started up, bumped along clucking to itself like a chicken looking for a place to drop an egg. I rode it along to its next client's back door, then hopped out, legged it to a public screen booth and dialled Gully's number.

4

I caught him in a cab, just dropping in past a mixed-up view of city skyline tilting by in the background. His eyes bugged out like a Chihuahua when I told him—a de luxe feature of the four-year-old Cantor he always wore.

"Barney, you nuts?" He had a yelp like a Chihuahua too. "The biggest bout of your career coming up tonight, and you're mixing in a free brawl!" He stopped to gulp and ran his eyes over me. "Hey, Barney! You're wearing an Arcaro. You didn't——"

"The fracas wasn't my idea," I got in quick while he was fightiig the Cantor's tonsils back in line. "Not exactly, anyway. I took off out the back way, and——"

"You did *what*?" The yelp was up into the supersonic now.

"I beat it. Ducked out. Scrammed. What do you think I was going to do, stay there and let that elbow squad pull the legs off me like a fly?"

"You can't run out on a registered satisfaction, Barney!" Gully leaned into his slender until all I could see were two eyes like bloodshot clams and a pair of quivering nostrils. "You, of all people! If the Pictonews services get hold of this, they'll murder you!"

15

"This hit squad will murder me quicker—and not just on paper!"

"Paper's what I'm talking about! You're the aggressor party; you poked the schlock! You cop a swiftie on this, and you're a fugitive from Law Cent! They'll lift your Servo license, and it'll be good-by career! And the fines——"

"Okay—but I got a few rights too! If I can get to another Servo before they grab me, it'll become my legal *Corpus operandi* as soon as I'm in it. Remember, that Satisfaction is to me, Barney Rum, not to this body I'm wearing. You've got to get me out of here, and back to my apartment——" I felt my mouth freeze in the open position. Fifty feet away across the Fastwalk the Liston and a new heavy, a big, patched-up Baer, had come out of a doorway and were standing there, looking over the crowd. Those boys were as hard to shake loose as gum on a shoe sole. I ducked down in the booth.

"Listen, Gully," I hissed. "They're too close; I've got to do a fast fade. Try to fix it with the Law Cent to keep their mitts off me until I can change. Remember, if they catch me, you can kiss your ten percent good-by."

"Barney, where you going? Whattaya mean, ten percent? It ain't the cookies I'm thinking about!"

"Think about the cookies, Gully." I cut contact and risked a peek. The two goons were still there and looking my way. If I stepped out, they'd have me. And if I stayed where I was, sooner or later they'd get around to checking the booth. . . .

I was still holding something in my hand. I looked at it: the cosmetics kit I'd grabbed on the way out of the ladies' room at the Troc.

The lid flipped back when I touched the little gold button at the side. There were nine shades of eye shadow, mouth paint, plastic lens shades in gold, green and pink—some dames have got screwy ideas about what looks attractive—spare eyebrows and lashes, a little emergency face putty, some thimble-sized hair sprays.

I hated to ruin a hundred cee wig, but I gave it a full shot of something called Silver Ghost. The pink eyes seemed to go with the hair. The spray was all gone, so it was too late to bleach out a set of eyebrows, so I used a pair of high-arched black ones, then used a gingery set for a mustache. I thought about using one of the fake spit curls for a goatee, but decided against it. The Arcaro had a nice-sized nose on it, so I widened the nostrils a little and added warts. I risked another peek. The boys were right where I left them.

My jacket was a nice chartreuse job with cerise strips and a solid orange lining. I turned it inside out, ditched the yellow tie, and opened my shirt collar so the violet part showed. That was about all I could do; I opened the door and stepped out.

I'd gone about three steps when the Carnera looked my way. His mouth dropped open like a power shovel getting ready to take a bit out of a hillside. He jammed an elbow into the Liston and he turned around and *his* mouth fell open. I got a glimpse of some nice white choppers and a tongue like a pink sock. I didn't wait to catch the rest of the reaction: I sprinted for the nearest shelter, a pair of swinging doors, just opening to let a fat Orggie out.

I dived past him into a cool, dark room lit by a couple of glowing beer ads above a long mirror with a row of bottles. I charged past all that, slammed through a door at the back, and was out in an alley, looking at the Wayne. He went into a half-crouch and spread his arms. That was the kind of mistake an amateur toughie would make. I put my head down and hit him square under his vest button. It wasn't the best treatment in the world for the Arcaro, but it was worse for the Wayne. He froze up and made a noise like frying fat, with his eyeballs spinning like Las Vegas cherries. Between the fall in the john and the butt in the neuro center, he was through for the day.

I got my legs under me and started off at a sort of cripple's lope toward the end of the alley.

My balance and coordination units were clicking like castanets. I richocheted off a couple of walls, made it out into the Slowwalk, and jigged along in a crabbed semicircle, making jerky motions with my good arm at a cab that picked then to drop a fare a few yards away. The hackie reached out, grabbed my shoulder and hauled me

17

inside. Those boys may be built into their seats and end at the waist, but they've got an arm on them. I'll give 'em that.

"You look like you got a problem there, Mac." He looked me over in the mirror. "What happened, you fall off a roof?"

"Something like that. Just take me to the Banshire Building, fast."

"Whatever you say, Bud. But if I was you, I'd get that Servo to a shop as quick as I could."

"Later. Step on it."

"I'm doing a max and a half now!"

"Okay, okay, just don't waste any time." He muttered to himself then, while I got the bent cover off my reset panel and did what I could to rebalance my circuitry. My double vision cleared a little, and the leg coordination improved enough so I managed to climb out unassisted when he slammed the heli in hard on the roof deck.

"Be five cees," the cabbie grunted. I paid him. "Stick around a few minutes," I said. "I'll be right back."

"Do me a favor, Clyde; throw your trade to the competition." He flipped the flag up and lifted off in a cyclone of overrevved rotors. I spat out a mouthful of grit and went in through the fancy door with the big gold B.

Gus, the doorman, came out of his cage with his admiral's hat on crooked; he hooked a thumb over his shoulder and got his jaw all set for the snappy line. I beat him to it.

"It's me, Barney Ramm. I'm incommunicado to avoid the fans."

"Geeze, Mr. Ramm? Wow, that Arcaro won't never be the same again. Looks like your fans must of caught you after all." He showed me a bunch of teeth that would have looked at home in a mule's face. I lifted a lip at him and went on in.

5

My apartment wasn't the plushest one in the Banshire, but it was fully equipped. The Servo stall was the equal of anything at Municipal Files. I got enough cooperation out of my legs to hobble to it, got the Arcaro into the rack with the neck plate open and the contacts tight against the transfer disk.

A pull on the locking lever, and I was clamped in tight, ready for the shift. I picked the Crockett; it was rugged enough to handle the Sullivan, and didn't have any fancy equipment installed to have to look out for. It was a little tough coding the number into the panel, but I made it, then slammed the transfer switch.

I've never gotten used to that wild couple of seconds while the high-speed scanner is stripping the stored data off one control matrix and printing it on another one linking it in to the Org brain back between my real ears in the cold files downtown. It was like diving into an ocean of ice-cold darkness, spinning like a Roman candle. All kinds of data bits flash through the conscious level: I was the Arcaro, sitting rigid in the chair, and I was also the Crockett, clamped to a rack in the closet, and at the same time I could feel the skull contacts and servicing tubes and the cold slab under me in the Vault. Then it cleared and I was hitting the release lever and stepping out of the closet and beginning to feel like a million bucks.

The Arcaro looked pretty bad, sagging in the stall, with the phony eyebrows out of line and the putty nose squashed, and the right shoulder humped up like Quasimodo. It was a wonder it had gotten me back at all. I made myself a promise to give it the best overhaul job money could buy—that was the least I could do. Then I headed for the front door.

The Sullivai would get a little surprise when I found him now. I gave my coon skin cap a pat as I went by the hall mirror, palmed the flush panel open and ran smack into four large cops, standing there waiting for me.

It was a plush jailhouse, as jails go, but I still didn't like it. They shoved me into a nice corner cell with a carpet, a tiled lube cubicle in the corner, and a window with a swell view of Granyauck—about 1800 feet straight down. There were no bars, but the wall was smooth enough to discourage any human flies from trying it.

The turnkey looked me over and shook his head. He

wearing the regulation Police Special, a dumb-looking production job halfway between a Kildare and a Tracy—Spence, that is. I guess cops have to have a uniform, but the sight of a couple dozen identical twins standing around kind of gives a fellow a funny feeling—like Servos were just some kind of robot, or something.

"So you're Barney Ramm, huh?" the cop shifted his toothpick to the other corner of his mouth. "You shunt of tried to handle four cops at once, Buddy. Your collision insurance don't cover that kind of damage."

"I want my manager!" I yelled as loud as I could, which wasn't very loud on account of a kick in the voice box I got following up too close on a cop I had tossed on his ear. "You can't do this to me! I'll get the lot of you for false arrest!"

"Relax, Ramm." The jailer waved his power-billie at me to remind me he had it. I shied off; a shot from the hot end of that would lock my neuro center in a hard knot. "You ain't going no place for a while," the cop stated. "Commissioner Malone wouldn't like it."

"Malone? The Arena Commissioner? What's he got ——" I stopped in the middle of the yell, feeling my silly look freeze in place.

"Yeah," the cop said. "Also the Police Commissioner. Seems like Malone don't like you, Ramm."

"Hey!" a dirty idea was growing. "The satisfaction against me: who filed it?"

The cop went through the motions of yawning. "Lessee . . . oh, yeah. A Mr. Malone."

"The dirty crook! That's illegal! I was framed!"

"You slugged him first, right?" The cop cut me off.

"Sure, but——"

"Ain't a Police Commissioner got as much right as anybody else to defend hisself? Any reason he's got to take guff off some wisenheimer, any more than the next guy? You race him at the light, he'll lock bumpers with you every time!"

"I've got to get out of here," I shouted him down. "Get Gully Fishbein! He'll post the bond! I've got a bout at the

20

Garden in less than four hours! Tell the judge! I guess I've got a couple rights!"

"You ain't going to make no bout in no four hours." The cop grinned like Sears foreclosing on Roebuck. "You'll be lucky if you get out before Christmas Holidays start, in September."

"If I don't," I said, "you can start scanning the help-wanted-cripple column. That's what you'll be when me and my twenty-thousand Cee Charlemagne finish with you, you dumb flatfoot!"

He narrowed his eyes down to pinpoints—an extra-cost feature that the taxpayers had to spring for. "Threats, hah?" His voice had the old gravel in it now. "You run out on a Satisfaction, Buster. That's trouble enough for most guys."

"I'll show you trouble," I started, but he wasn't through yet.

" . . . For a big tough arena fighter, you got kind of a delicate stomach, I guess. We also got you for resisting arrest, damaging public property, committing mayhem on the person of a couple honest citizens, Peeping Tom and shoplifting from the ladies' john. You're set for tonight, pal—and a lotta other nights." He gave me a mock salute and backed out; the glass door clinked in my face while I was still trying to get my arm back for a swing.

The watch set in my left wrist was smashed flat, along with the knuckles. Those Granyauck cops have got hard heads. I went over to the window and checked the sun.

It looked like about half past four. At eight P.M. the main event would go on. If I wasn't there, the challenger would take the title by default. He was an out-of-town phony known as Mysterious Marvin, the Hooded Holocaust; he always fought with a flour sack over his face. After tonight, he'd be light-heavy champ, bagged head and all—and I'd be a busted has-been, with my accounts frozen, my contract torn up, my Servo ticket lifted, and about as much future as a fifth of Bourbon at a Baptist Retreat. It was the finish. They had me. Unless . . .

I poked my head out and looked down the wall. It was

21

a sheer drop to a concrete loading apron that looked about the size of a blowout patch from where I stood. I felt my autonomics kick in; my heart started thumping like an out-of-round drive shaft, and my throat closed up like a crap-shooter's fist. I never had liked heights much. But with my Servo locked in a cell—and *me* locked in the Servo——

I took a couple turns up and down the cell. It was an idea the boys talked about sometimes, waiting in the service racks before a bout: what would happen if the plastic-foam and wire-sponge information correlation unit where the whole brain pattern was recorded got smashed flat—wiped out—while you were in it?

It would be like dreaming you fell—and hit. Would you ever wake up? The Org body was safe, back in the Vaults, but the shock—what would it do to you?

There were a lot of theories. Some of the guys said it would be curtains. The end. Some of them said your Org would go catatonic. I didn't know, myself. If the wheels knew, they weren't spreading it around.

And there was just the one way to find out for sure.

If I stayed where I was, incommunicado, I was finished anyway. Better to go out in style. Before I could change my mind, I whirled, went to the window and swung my legs over the sill. Behind me, I heard somebody yell, "Hey!" I tried to swallow, couldn't, squeezed my eyes shut and jumped. For a few seconds, it was like a tornado blowing straight up into my face; then it was like being spread-eagled on a big, soft, rubbery mattress. And then——

6

I was drowning in a sea of rancid fat. I took a deep breath to yell, and the grease in my lungs clogged solid.

I tried to cough and couldn't do that either. Little red skyrockets started shooting around back of my eyes like a fire in a fireworks factory. Then the lights ran together and I was staring at a long red glare strip set in a dark ceiling a few inches above my face. I could feel tubes and wires dragging at my arms and legs, my neck, my eyelids, my tongue . . .

I was moving, sliding out into brighter light. A scared-looking face was gaping down at me. I made gargly noises and flapped my hands—about all I could manage under the load of spaghetti. The guy leaning over me jumped like a morgue attendant seeing one of his customers sit up and ask for a light, which wasn't too far off, maybe. My bet had paid off. I was awake, back in my organic body in slot number 99971-Ga8b in the Municipal Body Files.

The next half hour was a little hectic. First they started some kind of a pump, and then I could breathe—a little. While I coughed, twitched, groaned, itched, throbbed and ached in more places than I knew I had, the file techs fussed over me like midwives delivering a TV baby. They pulled things out, stuck things in, sprayed me, jabbed me, tapped and tested, conferred, complained, ran back and forth, shone lights in my eyes, hit me with little hammers, poked things down my throat, held buzzers to my ears, asked questions and bitched at each other in high, whining voices like blue-bottle flies around a honey wagon. I got the general idea. They were unhappy that I had upset the routine by coming out of a stage-three storage state unannounced.

"There are laws against this sort of thing!" a dancey little bird in an unhealthy-looking Org body kept yelling at me. "You might have died! It was sheer good fortune that I happened to have slipped back in the stacks to commune with myself, and heard you choking! You frightened me out of my wits!"

Somebody else shoved a clipboard in front of me. "Sign this," he said. "It's a release covering Cent Files against any malpractice or damage claims."

"And there'll be an extra service charge on your file for emergency reprocessing," the dancey one said. "You'll have to sign that, and also an authorization to transfer you to dead storage until your next of kin or authorized agent brings in the Servo data——"

I managed to sit up. "Skip the reprocessing," I said. "And the dead storage. Just get me on my feet and show me the door."

"How's that? You're going to need at least a week's rest, a month's retraining, and a complete reorientation course before you can be released in Org——"

"Get me some clothes," I said. "Then I'll sign the papers."

"This is blackmail!" Dancey did a couple of steps. "I won't be held responsible!"

"Not if you cooperate. Call me a cab." I tried walking. I was shaky, but all things considered I didn' feel too bad—for a guy who just committed suicide. Files had kept me in good condition.

There was a little more argument, but I won. Dancey followed me out, wagging his head and complaining, but I signed his papers and he disappeared—probably to finish communing with himself.

In the cab, I tried to reach Gully again. His line was busy. I tried Lorena. A canned voice told me her line was disconnected. Swell. All my old associates were kind of fading out of sight, now that I was having troubles with the law.

But maybe Gully was just busy getting me a postponement. In fact, he was probably over at the Garden now, straightening things out. I gave the hackie directions and he dropped me by the big stone arch with the deep-cut letters that said FIGHTERS ENTRANCE.

The usual crowd of fight fans were there, forty deep. None of them gave me a look; they had their eyes on the big, wide-shouldered Tunneys and Louises and Marcianos, and the hammed-up Herkys and Tarzans in their flashy costumes and big smiles, with their handlers herding them along like tugs nudging liners into dock. The gateman put out a hand to stop me when I started through the turnstile.

"It's me, Harley. Barney Ramm," I said. A couple of harness cops were standing a few feet away, looking things over. "Let me through; I'm late."

"Hah? Barney——"

"Keep it quiet; I'm a surprise."

"Where'd you dig up that outfit? On a used-Servo lot?" He looked me over like an inspector rejecting a wormy side of mutton. "What is it, a gag?"

"It's a long story. I'll tell it to you some time. Right now, how's about loaning me a temporary tag? I left my ID in my other pants."

"You pugs," he muttered, but he handed over the pass. I grabbed it.

"Where's Lou Mitch, the starter?" I asked him.

"Try the Registry Office."

I shoved through a crowd of weigh-in men, service techs and arena officials, spotted Lou talking to a couple of trainers. I went over and grabbed his arm.

"It's me, Mitch, Barney Ramm. Listen, where's Gully? I need——"

"Ramm, you bum! Where you been? Where'd you pick up that hulk you got on? Who you think you are, missing the press weigh-in? Get downstairs on the double and dress out! You got twenty minutes, and if you're late, so help me, I'll see you busted out of the fight game!"

"Wha—who, me? Hold it, Lou, I'm not going out there in this condition! I just came down to——"

"Oh, a holdup for more dough, huh? Well, you can work that one out with the promoter and the Commissioner. All I know is, you got a contract, and I've got you billed for nineteen minutes from now!"

I started backing away, shaking my head. "Wait a minute, Lou——"

He jerked his head at a couple of the trainers that were listening in. "Grab him and take him down to his stall and get him into his gear! Hustle it!"

I put up a brisk resistance, but it was all wasted effort. Ten minutes later I was standing in the chute, strapped into harness with knots tied in the straps for fit and a copy of the Afternoon Late Racing Special padding my helmet up off my ears, listening to the mob in the stands up above, yelling for the next kill. Me.

7

They can talk all they want about how sensitive and responsive a good Servo is, but there's nothing like flesh and blood for making you know you're in trouble.

My heart was kicking hard enough to jar the championship medal on my chest. My mouth was as dry as yesterday's cinnamon toast. I thought about making a fast getaway over the barrier fence, but there was nobody outside who'd be glad to see me except the cops; besides which, I had a mace in my right hand and a fighting net in the left, and after all, I was Barney Ramm, the champ. I'd always said it was the man inside the Servo, not the equipment that counted. Tonight I had a chance to prove it—or a kind of a chance; an Org up against a fighting Servo wasn't exactly an even match.

But hell, when was it ever even? The whole fight game was controlled, from top to bottom, by a few sharpies like J. J. Malone. Nobody had ever slipped me the word to take a dive yet, but I'd stretched plenty of bouts to make 'em look good. After all, the fans paid good creds to see two fine-tuned fighting machines pound each other to scrap under the lights. An easy win was taboo. Well, they'd get an unexpected bonus tonight when I got hit and something besides hydraulic fluid ran out.

And then the blast of the bugles caught me like a bucket of ice water and the gate jumped up and I was striding through, head up, trying to look as arrogant as a hunting tiger under the glare of the polyarcs, but feeling very small and very breakable and wondering why I hadn't stayed in that nice safe jail while I had the chance. Out across the spread of the arena the bleachers rose up dark under the high late-evening sky streaked with long pink clouds that looked as remote as fairyland. And under the pooled lights, a big husky Servo was taking his bows, swirling his cloak.

He was too far away, over beyond the raised disk of the Circle, for me to be sure, but it looked like he was picking a heavy duty prod and nothing else. Maybe the word had gone out and I was in Org, or maybe he was good.

Then he tossed the cape to a handler and came to meet me, sizing me up on the way through the slit in his mask.

Maybe he was wondering what I had up my sleeve. If he was in on the fix, he'd be surprised to see me at all. He'd been expecting a last-minute sub or just a straight

26

default. If not, he'd have been figuring on me wearing my Big Charley packed with all the booster gear the law allows. Instead, all he saw was an ordinary-looking five-foot-eleven frame with medium-fair shoulders and maybe just a shade too much padding at the belt line.

The boys back at Files had done right by me, I had to admit. The old Org was in better shape than when I'd filed it, over a year ago. I felt strong, tough and light on my feet; I could feel the old fighting edge coming on. Maybe it was just a false lift from the stuff the techs had loaded me full of, and maybe it was just an animal's combat instinct, an item they hadn't been able to dream up an accessory to imitate. Whatever it was, it was nice to have.

I reached the concrete edge of the Fighting Circle and stepped up on it and was looking across at the other fellow, only fifty feet away and now looking bigger than a Bolo Combat Unit. With the mask I wasn't sure, but he looked like a modified Norge Atlas. He was running through a fancy twirl routine with the prod, and the crowd was eating it up.

There was no law that said I had to wait for him to finish. I slid the mace down to rest solid in my palm with the thong riding tight above my wrist and gave the two-foot club a couple of practice swings. So much for the warmup. I flipped the net out into casting position with my left hand and moved in on him.

It wasn't like wearing a Servo; I could feel sweat running down my face and the air sighing in my lungs and the blood pumping through my muscles and veins. It was kind of a strange *alive* feeling—as if there was nothing between me and the sky and the earth and I was part of them and they were part of me. A funny feeling. A dangerous, un-protected feeling—but somehow not entirely a bad feeling.

He finished up the ham act when I was ten feet from him, swung to face me. He knew I was there, all right; he was just playing it cool. Swell. While he was playing, I'd take him.

I feinted with the net, then dived in, swung the mace, missed him by half an inch as he back-pedaled. I followed him close, working the club, keeping the net cocked. He

27

backed, looking me over.

"Ramm—is that you in that getup?" he barked.

"Naw—I couldn't make it, so I sent my cousin Julius."

"What happened, you switch brands? Looks like you must of got cut-rate merchandise." He ducked a straight cut and whipped the prod around in a jab that would have paralyzed my neuro center if he'd connected.

"New secret model a big outfit's trying out under wraps," I told him.

He made a fast move, and a long, slim rod I hadn't seen before whipped out and slapped me under the ribs. For a split second I froze. He had me, I was finished. A well-handled magnetic resonator could deGauss every micro-tape in a Servo—and his placement was perfect.

But nothing happened. There was a little tingle, that was all.

Then I got it. I wasn't wearing a Servo—and magnets didn't bother an Org.

The Atlas was looking as confused as I was. He took an extra half-second recovering. That was almost enough. I clipped him across the thigh as he almost fell getting back. He tried with the switch again, sawed it across my chest. I let him; he might as well tickle me with a grass stem. This time I got the net out, snarled his left arm, brought the mace around and laid a good one across his hip. It staggered him, but he managed to spin out, flip the net clear.

"What kind of shielding you got anyway, Ramm?" the Atlas growled. He held the rod out in front of his face, crossed his eyes at it, shook it hard and made one more try. I let him come in under my guard, and the shaft slid along my side as if he was trying to wipe it clean on my shirt. While he was busy with that, I dropped the net, got a two-handed grip in the mace, brought it around in a flat arc and laid a solid wallop right where it would do him the most good—square on the hip joint.

I heard the socket go. He tried to pivot on his good leg, tottered and just managed to stay on his feet, swearing. I came in fast and just got a glimpse of the electro-pod coming up. Concentrating on the magnetic rod, I'd forgotten the other. I tried to check and slide off to the right, but

28

all of a sudden blinding blue lights were popping all over the sky. Something came up and hit me alongside the head, and then I was doing slow somersaults through pretty purple clouds, trying hard to figure which side was up. Then the pain hit. For a couple of seconds I scraped at my chest, reaching for circuit breakers that weren't there. Then I got mad.

It was as if all of a sudden, nothing could stop me. The Atlas was a target, and all I wanted was just to reach it. If there was a mountain in the way, I'd pick it up and throw it over my shoulder. A charging elephant would be a minor nuisance. I could even stand up, unassisted—if I tried hard enough.

I got the feel of something solid under my hands, groped and found some more of it with my feet, pushed hard and blinked away the fog to see the Atlas just making it back onto his good leg. I had to rest a while then, on all fours. He stooped to twiddle a reset for emergency power to the damaged joint, then started for me, hopping hard enough to shake the ground. A little voice told me to wait.
. . .

He stopped, swung the prod up, and I rolled, grabbed his good leg, twisted with everything I had. It wasn't enough. He hopped, jabbed with the prod, missed, and I was on my feet now, feeling like I'd been skinned and soaked in brine. My breath burned my throat like a blow torch, and all round the crowd roar was like a tidal wave rolling across a sinking continent.

I backed, and he followed. I tried to figure the time until the pit stop, but I didn't know how long I'd been out here; I didn't have a timer ticking under my left ear, keeping me posted. And now the Atlas was on to what was going on. I knew that, when he reached for the show-knife strapped to his left hip. Against a Servo, that particular tool was useless, but he could let the cool night air into an Org's gizzard with it, and he knew it.

Then my foot hit the edge of the paved circle and I went down, flat on my back on the sand.

The Atlas came after me, and I scrambled back, got to
29

my feet just in time. The knifeblade hissed through the air just under my chin.

"You've had it, Ramm," the Atlas said, and swung again. I tried to get the club up for a counterblow but it was too heavy. I let it drop and drag in the sand. Through a dust cloud we were making, I saw the Atlas fumbling with his control buttons. Tears welled up in his eyes, sluiced down over his face. He didn't like the dust any better than I did. Maybe not as well . . .

I felt an idea pecking at its shell; a dirty idea, but better than none.

The mace was dangling by its thong. I slipped it free, threw it at him; it clanged off his knees and I stooped, came up with a handful of fine sand and as he closed in threw it straight into his face.

The effect was striking. His eyes turned to mud pockets. I stepped aside, and he went right past me, making swipes at the air with the big sticker, and I swung in behind him and tilted another handful down inside his neckband. I could hear it grate in the articulated rib armor as he came around.

"Ramm, you lousy little——" I took aim and placed a nice gob square in his vocabulary. He backed off, pumping emergency air to clear the pipes, spouting dust like Mount Aetna, but I knew I had him. The mouth cavity on just about every Servo in the market was a major lube duct; he had enough grit in his gears to stop a Continental Siege Unit. But his mouth was still open, so I funneled in another double handful.

He stopped, locked his knee joints and concentrated on his problem. That gave me my opening to reach out and switch his main circuit breaker off.

He froze. I waited half a minute for the dust to clear, while the crowd roar died away to a kind of confused buzzing, like robbed bees.

Then I reached out, put a finger against his chest, and shoved—just gently. He leaned back, teetered for a second, then toppled over stiff as a lamppost. You could hear the thud all the way to the student bleachers. I held on for another ten seconds, just to make it look good, then kneeled over on top of him.

8

"But I was too late," Gully Fishbein's voice was coming up out of a barrel, a barrel full of thick molasses syrup somebody had dumped me into. I opened my mouth to complain and a noise like "glug" came out.

"He's awake!" Gully yelped. I started to deny it, but the effort was too much.

"Barney, I tried to catch you, but you were already out there." Gully sounded indignant. "Cripes, kid, you should of known I wouldn't let 'em railroad you!"

"Don't worry about Ramm," a breezy voice jostled Gully's aside. "Boy, this is the story of the decade! You figure to go up against a Servo again in Org, when you get out of the shop—I mean hospital? How did it feel to take five thousand volts of DC? You know the experts say it should have killed you. It would have knocked out any Servo on the market——"

"Nix, Baby!" Gully elbowed his way back in again. "My boy's gotta rest. And you can tell the world the Combo's out of business. Now anybody can afford to fight. Me and Barney have put the game back in the hands of the people."

"Yeah! The sight of that Atlas, out on its feet—and Ramm here, in Org, yet, with one finger. . . ."

I unglued an eyelid and blinked at half a dozen fuzzy faces like custard pies floating around me.

"We'll talk contract with you, Fishbein," somebody said.

". . . . call for some new regulations," somebody said.

". . . . dred thousand cees, first network rights."

". . . . era of the Servo in the arena is over . . ."

". . . . hear what Malone says about this. Wow!"

"Malone," I heard my voice say, like a boot coming out of mud. "The cr . . . crook. It was him . . . put the Sullivan . . . up to it . . . "

"Up to nothing, Barney," Gully was bending over me. "That was J. J. hisself in that Servo! And here's the payoff. He registered the Satisfaction in his own name—and of course, every fighter in his stable is acting in his name, legally. So when you met Mysterious Marvin and knocked him on his duff you satisfied his claim. You're in the clear, kid. You can relax. There's nothing to worry about."

"Oh, Barney!" It was a new voice, a nice soft little squeal of a girl-voice. A neat little Org face with a turned-up nose zeroed in on me, with a worried look in the big brown eyes.

"Julie! Where—I mean, how . . . ?"

"I was there, Barney. I see all your fights, even if —even if I don't approve. And today—oh, Barney, you were so brave, so *marvelous,* out there alone, against that *machine* . . . " She sighed and nestled her head against my shoulder.

"Gully," I said. "Exactly how long have I got to stay in this place?"

"The Servo-tech—I mean the doc—says a week anyway."

"Set up a wedding for a week from today."

Julie jumped and stared at me.

"Oh, Barney! But you—you know what I said . . . about those *zombies* . . . ."

"I know."

"But, Barney . . ." Gully didn't know whether to cry or grin. "You mean . . . ?"

"Sell my Servos," I said. "The whole wardrobe. My days of being a pair of TV eyes peeking out of a walking dummy and kidding myself I'm alive are over."

"Yeah, but Barney—a guy with your ideas about what's fun—like skiing, and riding the jetboards, and surfing, and sky-diving—you can't take the risks! You only got the one Org body!"

"I found out a couple of things out there tonight, Gully. It takes a live appetite to make a meal a feast. From now on, whatever I do, it'll be *me* doing it. Clocking records is okay, I guess, but there's some things that it takes an Org to handle."

"Like what?" Gully yelled, and went on with a lot more in the same vein. I wasn't listening, though. I was too busy savoring a pair of warm, soft, *live* lips against mine.

THE PLANET WRECKERS

1

In his shabby room in the formerly elegant hostelry known as the Grand Atumpquah Palace, Jack Waverly pulled the coarse weave sheet up about his ears and composed himself for sleep.

Somewhere, a voice whispered. Somewhere, boards creaked. Wind muttered around the loosely fitted window, rattling it in its frame. The pulled-down blind clacked restlessly. In the room above, footsteps went three paces; clank; back three paces; clank . . . .

Drat the fellow, Waverly thought. *Why doesn't he stop rattling his chains and go to bed?* He turned on his other side, rearranged the pillow of the consistency of bagged sawdust. Beyond the partition, someone was whistling a strange, unmelodic tune. It was hot in the room. The sheet chafed his neck. Next door, voices muttered with a note of urgency. Waverly made out the words *magma* and *San Andreas fault.*

"Geology, at ten minutes past midnight?" he inquired of the mottled wallpaper. Above, bedsprings squeaked faintly. Waverly sat up, frowning at the ceiling. "I thought the clerk said he was putting me on the top floor," he said accusingly. He reached for the telephone on the bedside table. A wavering dial tone went on for five seconds, then cut off with a sharp click.

"Hello?" Waverly said. "Hello?"

The receiver was dead against his ear.

"If this weren't the only hotel in town," Waverly muttered.

He climbed out of bed, went to the high window, raised the roller shade, looked out on a view of a brick wall ten

33

feet away. From the window next door, a pattern of light and shadow gleamed against the masonry.

Two silhouettes moved. One was tall, lean, long-armed, like a giant bird with a crested head and curious wattles below a stunted beak. The other resembled an inverted polyp, waving a dozen arms tipped with multifingered hands, several of which clutched smoking cigars.

"Trick of the light," Waverly said firmly. He closed his eyes and shook his head to dispel the illusion. When he looked again, the window was dark.

"There, you see?" He raised the sash and thrust his head out. Moonlight gleamed on a bricked alley far below. A rusted fire escape led upward toward the roof. Leaning far out, Waverly saw the sill of the window above.

"No lights up there," he advised himself. "Hmmmm."

Faintly, he heard a dull rattle of metal, followed by a lugubrious groan.

"True, it's none of your business," he said. "But inasmuch as you can't sleep anyway . . ." Waverly swung his legs over the sill onto the landing and started up.

As he reached the landing above, something white fluttered out at him. Waverly shied, then saw that it was a curtain, billowing out from an open window. Abruptly, a feminine sob sounded from within. He poked his head up far enough to peer over the window sill into darkness.

"Is, ah, something the matter?" he called softly. There was a long moment of silence.

"Who's there?" a dulcet female voice whispered.

"Waverly, madam, Jack Waverly. If I can be of any help?"

"Are you with the Service?"

"I'm with ISLC," Waverly said. He pronounced it as a word "islick." "That's International Sa——"

"Listen to me, Wivery," the voice was urgent. "Whatever he's paying you, I'll double it! And you'll find the Service not ungrateful."

"No payment is necessary for aid to damsels in distress," Waverly returned. "Er, may I come in?"

"Of couurse! Hurry up, before one of those slimy Gimps steps out for a stroll up the wall and sees you!"

34

Waverly climbed quickly in through the window. The room, he saw, was a mere garret, cramped under a low ceiling. It appeared to contain no furniture other than a dimly seen cot against one wall. A vague form moved a willowy arm there. Waverly moved toward it.

"You don't have a molecular disassociator with you?" the melodious voice queried urgently. "There's not much time left."

"Ah . . . no, I'm afraid not. I——"

"They mean to strap me to my own twifler, set the war-perators at two and a half busters and aim me toward Neptune," the feminine voice went on breathlessly. "Can you imagine anything more brutal?"

Waverly groped forward. "Now, now, my dear. Don't be upset."

As he reached the cot, his hand fell on stout links looped around the foot rail.

He fumbled, encountered the blocky shape of a hefty padlock.

"Good lord! I thought—that is, I didn't actually think——"

"That's right. Chained to the bed," there was a slight quaver in the voice.

"B-but—this is preposterous! It's criminal!"

"It's an indication of their desperation, Wivery! They've gone so far now that nothing short of the most drastic measures can stop them!"

"I think this is a matter for the authorities," Waverly blurted. "I'll put a call through immediately!"

"How? You can't get through."

"That's right; I'd forgotten about the phone."

"And anyway—I *am* the authorities," the soft voice said in a tone of utter discouragement.

"You? A mere slip of a girl?" Waverly's hand touched something cool, with the texture like nubbly nylon carpeting.

"I weighed three hundred and seventy pounds, Earth equatorial," the voice came back sharply. "And we Vorplischers happen to be a matriarchal society!"

A pale shape stirred, rose up from the rumpled bedding.

35

A head the size of a washtub smiled a footwide smile that was disconcertingly located above a pair of limpid brown eyes. A hand which appeared to be equipped with at least nine fingers reached up to pat a spongy mass of orange fibers matted across the top of the wide face. Waverly broke his paralysis sufficiently to utter a sharp yelp.

"Shhh!" the sweet voice issued from a point high in the chest. "I appreciate your admiration, but we don't want those monsters to hear you!"

2

"Fom Berj, Detective Third Class, at your service," the creature soothed Waverly. "I'm not supposed to reveal my identity, but under the circumstances I think it's only appropriate."

"D—delighted," Waverly choked. "Pardon my falling down. It's just that I was a trifle startled at your, ah, unusual appearance."

"It's perfectly understandable. A neat disguise, don't you think? I made it myself."

Waverly gulped. "Disguise?"

"Of course. You don't think this is my natural look, do you?"

Waverly laughed shakily. "I must confess that what with all this creeping around in the dark, I *was* ready to leap to conclusions." He peered at the massive form, more clearly visible now that his eyes accommodated to the dim light. "But what are you disguised as, if you don't mind my asking?"

"Why, as a native, of course. The same as you are, silly."

"As I am what?"

"Disguised as a native."

"Native of where?"

"Of this planet."

"Oh, of course." Waverly was backing toward the window. "Of this planet. A native . . . I take it you're from some *other* planet?"

The detective laughed a rippling laugh. "You have a jolly sense of humor, Wivery. As if a Vorplischer were native to this patch of wilderness."

"And the people who chained you up—are they from, ah, Vorplisch, too?" Waverly made conversation to cover his retreat.

"Don't be absurd. They're a mixed bag of Broogs, Limpicos, Erwalts, Glimps and Pud knows what-all." Fom Berj rattled her manacles. "We'd better do something about these chains in a hurry," she added briskly.

As Waverly reached the window, an eerie, purplish glow sprang up outside, accompanied by a shrill warbling. Waverly retreated hastily.

"I think that's them arriving with my twifler now," Fom Berj said tensely. "It's a brand-new model, equipped with the latest in antiac gear and the new infinite-capacity particle ingesters. You can imagine what *that* means! My frozen corpse will be three parsecs beyond Pluto before my Mayday beep clears the first boost station."

"Frozen corpse? Pluto?" Waverly gobbled.

"I know it sounds fantastic, but disposing of an agent of the Service is a mere bagatelle to these operators, compared with what they're planning!"

"What *are* they planning?" Waverly choked.

"Don't you know? I thought you were working for Izlik."

"Well, he, ah, doesn't tell us much. . . ."

"Mmmm. I don't know about that Izlik. Sometimes I wonder just how deep a game he's playing. By the way, where *is* he?"

"He was delayed by a heavy cloud cover over Ypsilanti," Waverly improvised. "He'll be along later." His eyes roved the room, searching for an escape route. "You were saying?" he prompted in an obscure instinct to keep the detective talking.

"They're making a Galacular," Fom Berj said solemnly.

"A . . . Galacular?"

"Now you see the extent of their madness. An open violation of Regulation 69723468b!"

There was a sharp series of bumping sounds above. "Better hurry with that molecular disassociator," Fom Berj said.

"What's a Galacular?" Waverly was close to the door now. He froze as something made a slithery sound beyond it.

"A multi-D thriller," Fom Berj was explaining. "You know, one of those planetary debacle epics."

"What sort of debacle?" Waverly recoiled at a sound as of heavy breathing outside the door.

"Floods, quakes, typhoons—you know the sort of thing. Audiences love them, in spite of their illegality. The first scene they're shooting tonight will be a full-scale meteor strike in a place called Montana."

"You mean—a *real* meteor?"

"Of course. According to my informant, they've grappled onto a cubic mile or so of nickel-iron that was parked in a convenient orbit a few million miles out, and nudged it in this direction. I would have stopped it there, of course, but I blundered and they caught me," the detective sighed. "It should make quite an effective splash when it hits."

"They're going to wreck an entire state just for a—a spectacle?" Waverly choked.

"I see you're not familiar with the Galacular craze. To be accepted by discriminating multi-D fans, nothing less than a genuine disaster will serve."

Up above on the roof, heavy feet clumped; something massive bump-bumped.

Fom Berj's voice was icy calm. "Now, Wivery, it's true we Vorplischers pride ourselves on our coolness in the face of peril, but WILL YOU GET THESE DAMNED CHAINS OFF ME BEFORE IT'S TOO LATE!"

Waverly darted to the window. "Don't go away," he called over his shoulder. "I'll be right back!"

It took Waverly forty-five seconds to descend to his room, snatch up his sample case, hastily examine his tongue in the mirror and retrace his steps to the attic. He opened the case, lettered International Safe and Lock Corporation, took out a tool shaped like a miniature crochet hook, turned to the lock.

"Hmmm. A variation on the Katzenburger-McIlhenney patents," he muttered. "Child's play . . ." He probed

38

delicately in the wide key slot, frowning as he worked.

"Hurry, Wivery!" Fom Berj cried.

Waverly wiped perspiration from his forehead. "It's trickier than it looked," he said defensively. "Apparently they've employed a double-reserve cam action."

Feet clumped on stairs, descending from the roof. A mutter of hoarse voices sounded in the hall, just beyond the door. The latch rattled. Waverly reached for his sample case, rummaged among the odds and ends there, came up with a cylindrical object. He sprang to the door, hastily engaged the chain latch just as the doorknob turned cautiously. The door creaked, swung open two inches, came to rest against the chain. A beaklike nose appeared at the opening, followed by a hand holding a gun.

Aiming coolly, Waverly directed a jet of menthol shaving cream at a pair of close-set eyes just visible above the nose. They withdrew with a muffled shriek. The gun clattered on the floor. Waverly snatched up the weapon, jammed it in his waistband, dashed back to the lock. Five seconds later, it opened with a decisive *spongg!* Fom Berj emitted a delighted squeak, rolled off the bed as the chains clattered to the floor. Waverly gaped at the cluster of supple members on which the bulky detective rippled swiftly across to the window. Outside the door, excited twitters, burbles and growls sounded interrogatory notes. The doorknob rattled. Something heavy struck the door.

"To the roof!" Fom Berj flowed through the window and was gone. The door shook to a thunderous impact. Waverly sprang to the window. On the landing, he looked down. A round, pale face with eyes like bubbles in hot tar stared up at him. He yelped and dashed for the roof.

Pulling himself up over the parapet, Waverly looked across an expanse of starlit roof, at the center of which an object shaped like a twelve-foot gravy boat rested lightly on three spidery jacks. The upper half was a clear plastic, hinged open like a mussel shell. Fom Berj was halfway to it when a small, sharp-featured head appeared over its gunwale. The monkeylike face split vertically, emitted a sharp cry and dived over the side. The boat rocked perilously as Fom Berj swarmed up and in; she turned, extended a long, three-elbowed arm to Waverly, hauled

39

him up as something popped nearby. Pale chartreuse gas swirled about the canopy as it slammed down. The detective lurched to a small, green-plush-covered contour seat, groped for the controls. Waverly scrambled after her, found himself crowded into a restricted space which was apparently intended as a parcel shelf.

"Which way is Montana?" the detective inquired over a rising hum that sprang up as she poked buttons on the padded dash.

"Straight ahead, about a thousand miles," Waverly called.

"Hold on tight," Fom Berj cried as the little vehicle leaped straight up. "On optimum trajectory, the trip will take close to half an hour. I don't know if we'll be in time or not."

3

Level at 100,000 feet, the twifler hummed along smoothly, making the whispering sound which gave it its name. Its velocty was just under 1850 MPH.

"Hurry," Waverly urged.

"Any faster at this altitude and we'd ablate," Fom Berj pointed out. "Relax, Wivery. We're doing our best."

"How can I relax?" Waverly complained. "The headroom is grossly inadequate."

"Well, you know the Q-stress engine produces a lens-shaped field with a minor radius proportional to the reciprocal of the fourth power of the input. To give you room to stand up, we'd need a diameter of about half a light-year. That's unwieldy."

"Hmmm. I wondered why flying saucers were shaped like that. It never occurred——"

"It seems to me you're pretty ignorant of a lot of things," Fom Berj studied Waverly with one eye, keeping the other firmly fixed on the instrument panel.

"I seem to note certain deficiencies in your costume, when it comes to that," he pointed out somewhat acidly. He eyed the three padded foundation garments strapped around the bulbous torso. "Most local beauties consider two of *those* sufficient," he added.

40

"You don't know much about these locals. They're mammary-happy. And if two of a given organ are attractive, six are triply attractive."

"What are you trying to attract?"

"Nothing. But a girl likes to make a good impression."

"Speaking of impressions—what are you planning on doing about this meteorite? You *did* say a cubic mile?"

"I was hoping to disintegrate it outside the outer R-belt, if possible, but I'm afraid we're running a little late."

"A thing that size—" Waverly felt the sweat pop on his forehead—"will vaporize the crust of the earth for miles around the point of impact!"

"I hate to think of what it will do to the native wild life," Fom Berj said. "Their feeding and mating habits will be upset, their nests destroyed——" Fom Berj broke off. "Oh, dear, I'm afraid we're too late!"

Ahead, a glowing point had appeared high in the sky. It descended steadily, becoming rapidly brighter. Waverly braced his feet as the twifler decelerated sharply, veering off. The glaring point of fire was surrounded by a greenish aurora.

"It's about three hundred miles out, I'd say," Fom Berj commented. "That means it will strike in about thirty seconds."

A faint, fiery trail was visible now behind the new star. Through the clear plastic hatch, Waverly watched as a beam of blue light speared out from the swelling central fire, probed downward, boiling away a low cloud layer.

"What's that?" Waverly squeaked.

"A column of compressed gases. It will be splashing up a nice pit for the actual body to bury itself in."

A pink glow had sprung up from the surface far below. The approaching meteor was an intolerable point of brilliance now, illuminating the clouds like a full moon. The light grew brighter; now Waverly could see a visible diameter, heading the streaming tail of fire. Abruptly it separated into three separate fragments, which continued on parallel courses.

"Tsk," Fom Berj clucked. "It exploded. That means an even wider distribution . . ."

41

With appalling swiftness the three radiant bodies expanded to form a huge, irregular glob of brilliance, dropping swiftly now, darting downward as quick as thought——

The sky opened into a great fan of yellow light more vivid than the sun.

Waverly squinted at the actinic display, watched it spread outward, shot through with rising jets of glowing stuff, intersperse with rocketlike streaks that punched upward, higher, higher, and were gone from view—all in utter silence. The far horizons were touched with light now. Then, slowly, the glare faded back. The silver-etched edges of the clouds dimmed away, until only a great rosy glow in the west marked the point of the meteorite's impact.

"Fooey," Fom Berj said. "Round one to the opposition."

Waverly and the Vorplischer stared down at the mile-wide, white-hot pit bubbling fifty thousand feet below and ten miles ahead.

"You have to confess the rascals got some remarkable footage that time," Fom Berj commented.

"This is incredible!" Waverly groaned. "You people —whoever you are—were aware that this band of desperadoes planned this atrocity—and all you sent was one female to combat them?"

"I'll disregard the chauvinistic overtones of that remark," Fom Berj said severely, "and merely remind you that the Service is a small one, operating on a perennially meager appropriation."

"If your precious Service were any sort of interplanetary police force, it wouldn't tolerate this sort of sloppy work," Waverly said sharply.

"Police force? Where did you get an idea like that? I'm a private eye in the employ of the Game and Wildlife Service."

"Wildlife——" Waverly started.

"Brace yourself," Fom Berj said. "Here comes the shock wave."

The twifler gave a preliminary shudder, then wrenched

itself violently end-for-end, at the same time slamming violently upward, to the accompaniment of a great metalic *zonnggg!* of thunder.

"I shudder to imagine how that would have felt without the special antiac equipment," the detective gasped. "Now, if we expect to intercept these scoundrels in the act of shooting their next scene, there's no time to waste."

"You mean they're going to do it *again?*"

"Not the same routine, of course. This time they're staging a major earthquake in a province called California. They'll trigger it by beaming the deep substrata with tight-focus tractor probes. The whole area is in a delicate state of balance, so all it will take is the merest touch to start a crustal readjustment that will satisfy the most exacting fans."

"The San Andreas Fault," Waverly groaned. "Good-by, San Francisco!"

"It's the Sequoias I'm thinking of," Fom Berj sighed. "Remarkable organisms, and not nearly so easy to replace as San Franciscans."

4

The twifler hurtled across the Rockies at eighty thousand feet, began to let down over northwestern Nevada, an unbroken desert gleaming ghostly white in the light of a crescent moon. Far ahead, San Francisco glowed on the horizon.

"This gets a trifle tricky now," Fom Berj said. "The recording units will be orbiting the scene of the action at a substratospheric level, of course, catching it all with wide-spectrum senceivers, but the production crew will be on the ground, controlling the action. They're the ones we're after. And in order to capture these malefactors red-handed, we'll have to land and go in on foot for the pinch. That means leaving the protection of the twifler's antiac field."

"What will we do when we find them?"

"I'd prefer to merely lay them by the heels with a liberal application of stun gas. If they're alive to stand trial, the publicity will be a real bonus, careerwise.

43

However, it may be necessary to vaporize them."

Decelerating sharply, Fon Berj dropped low over the desert, scanning the instruments closely.

"They've shielded their force bubble pretty well," she said. "But I think I've picked it up." She pointed. Waverly detected a vague bluish point glowing on a high rooftop near the north edge of the city. "A good position, with an excellent view of the target area."

Waverly held on as the flier swooped, low, whistled in a tight arc and settled in on a dark rooftop. The hatch popped up, admitted a gust of cool night air. Waverly and the detective advanced to the parapet. A hundred yards distant across a bottomless, black chasm, the blue gow of the fifty-foot force bubble shone eerily. Waverly was beginning to sweat inside his purple pajamas.

"What if they see us?" he hissed—and dropped flat as a beam of green light sizzled past his head from the bubble and burst into flame.

"Does that answer your question?" Fom Berj was crouched behind the parapet. "Well, there's no help for it. I'll have to use sterner measures." She broke off as the deck underfoot trembled, then rose in a series of jarring jerks, dropped a foot, thrust upward again. A low rumble had started up. Brick came pelting down from adjacent buildings to smash thunderously below.

"Oh, oh, it's started!" Fom Berj shrilled. Clinging to the roof with her multiple ambulatory members, the detective unlimbered a device resembling a small fire extinguisher, took aim and fired. Waverly, bouncing like a passenger in a Model T Ford, saw a yellow spear of light dart out, glance off the force bubble and send up a shower of sparks as it scored the blue-glowing sphere.

"Bull's-eye!" Fom Berj trilled. "A couple more like that, and——"

The whole mountainside under the building seemed to tilt. The parapet toppled and was gone. Waverly grabbed for a stout TV antenna, held on as his feet swung over the edge. Fom Berj emitted a sharp scream and grabbed for a handhold. The vaporizer slid past Waverly, went over the edge.

"That does it," the detective cried over the roar of

44

crumbling mortar. "We tried, Wivery!"

"Look!" Waverly yelled. Over his shoulder, he saw the force bubble suddenly flicker violet, then green, then yellow—and abruptly dwindle to half its former diameter. Through a pall of dust, Waverly discerned the outlines of an elaborate apparatus resembling an oversized X-ray camera, now just outside the shrunken blue bubble. A pair of figures, one tall and thin, the other rotund and possessing four arms, dithered, scrabbling at the dome for entrance. One slipped and disappeared over the roof's edge with a mournful yowl. The other scampered off across the buckling roof, leaped to an adjacent one, disappeared in a cloud of smoke and dust.

"Did you see that?" Fom Berj cried. "They've had to abandon their grappler! We've beaten them!"

"Yes—but what about the earthquake?" Waverly called as the roof under him bounded and leaped.

"We'll just have to ride it out and hope for the best!"

Through the dust cloud, they watched as the blue bubble quivered, swam upward from its perch, leaving the abandoned tractor beamer perched forlornly on the roof.

"Let them go," Fom Berj called. "As soon as the ground stops shaking, we'll be after them."

Waverly looked out toward the vast sprawl of lights, which were now executing a slow, graceful shimmy. As he watched, a section of the city half a mile square went dark. A moment later, the twinkling oramge lights of fires sprang up here and there across the darkened portion. Beyond the city, the surface of the Pacific heaved and boiled. A dome swelled up, burst; green water streamed back as a gout of black smoke belched upward in a roiling fire-shot cloud. The moonlight gleamed on a twenty-foot wavefront that traveled outward from the submarine eruption. Waverly saw it meet and merge with the waterfront, sweep grandly inland, foaming majestically about the bases of the hills on which the city was built. The long, undulating span of the Golden Gate bridge wavered in a slow snake dance, then descended silently into the bay, disappeared in a rising smother of white. More light went out; more fires appeared across the rapidly darkening city.

A deafening rumble rolled continuously across the scene of devastation.

Now the backwash of the tidal wave was sweeping back out to sea, bearing with it a flotsam of bars, billboards, seafood restaurants and automobiles, many of the latter with their headlights still on, gleaming murkily through the shallow waters. Smoke was forming a pall across the mile of darkened ruins, lit from beneath by leaping flames. Here and there the quick yellow flashes of explosions punctuated the general overcast.

"G-good Lord," Waverly gasped as the shaking under him subsided into a quiver and then was still. "What an incredible catastrophe!"

"That was nothing to what it would have been if they'd had time to give it a good push," Fom Berj commented.

"The fiends!" Waverly scrambled to his feet. "Some of the best bars in the country were down there!"

"It could have been worse."

"I suppose so. At least the San Franciscans are used to it. Imagine what that tidal wave would have done to Manhattan!"

"Thanks for reminding me," Fom Berj said. "That's where the next scene is due to be shot."

5

"The scare we gave them should throw them far enough behind schedule to give us a decent crack at them this time," Fom Berj said, staring forward into the night as the twifler rocketed eastward. "Thes only have the one production unit here, you know. It's a shoestring operation, barely a hundred billion dollar budget."

Waverly, crouched again in his cramped perch behind the pilot, peered out as the lights of Chicago appeared ahead, spread below them and dwindled behind.

"What do they have in mind for New York? Another earthquake? A fire? Or maybe just a super typhoon?"

"Those minor disturbances won't do for this one," Fom Berj corrected him. "This is the climactic scene of the show. They plan to collapse a massive off-shore igneous dike and let the whole stretch of continental shelf from

46

Boston to Cape Charles slide into the ocean."

"Saints preserve us!" Waverly cried.

"You should see what they'd do on a Class-A budget," Fom Berj retorted. "The local moon would look quite impressive, colliding with Earth."

"Ye gods! You sound almost as if you approve of these atrocities!"

"Well, I used to be a regular Saturday-afternoon theatergoer; but now that I've attained responsible age, I see the folly of wasting planets that way."

The blaze of lights that was the Atlantic seaboard swam over the horizon ahead, rushed toward the speeding twifler.

"They're set up on a barg about five miles off-shore," the detective said as they swept over the city. "It's just a little field rig; it will only be used once of course." She leaned forward. "Ah, there it is now!"

Waverly gaped at a raft of lights visible on the sea ahead.

"Gad!" he cried. "The thing's the size of a Australian sheep ranch!"

"They need a certain area on which to set up the antenna arrays," Fom Berj said. "After all, they'll be handling a hundred billion megavolt-seconds of power. Now, we'll just stand off at about twenty miles and lob a few rounds into them. I concede it will be a little messy, what with the initial flash, the shock wave, the fallout and the storms and tidal waves, but it's better than letting them get away."

"Wait a minute—your cure sounds as bad as the disease! We're a couple of miles from the most densely populated section of the country! You'll annihilate thousands!"

"You really *are* hipped on conservation," Fom Berj said. "However, you can't cure tentacle mildew without trimming off a few tentacles. Here goes . . ."

"No!" Waverly grabbed for the detective's long arm as the latter placed a spatulate finger on a large pink button. Taken by surprise, Fom Berj yanked the limb back, struck a lever with her elbow. At once, the canopy snapped up and was instantly ripped away by the hundred-mile-per-hour slipstream. Icy wind tore at Waverly's pajamas, shrieked past his face, sucked the air from his lungs. Fom Berj grabbed for the controls, fought the bucking twifler as it went into a spin, hurtling down toward the black surface of the sea.

"Wivery! I can't hold it! Vertigo! Take over . . . ." Waverly barely caught the words before the massive body of the feminine detective slumped and slid down under the dash. He reached, caught the wildly vibrating control tiller, put all his strength into hauling it back into line. The flier tilted, performed an outside loop followed by a snap-roll. Only Waverly's safety harness prevented him from being thrown from the cockpit. He shoved hard on the tiller, and the twifler went into a graceful inverted chandelle. Waverly looked "up," saw a vast spread of dark-glittering, white-capped ocean slowly tilting over him. With a convulsive wrench of the tiller he brought the Atlantic down and under his keel and was racing along fifty feet above the water. He dashed the wind-tears from his eyes, saw the lights of the barge rushing at him, gave a convulsive stab at four buttons at random and squeezed his eyes shut.

The twifler veered sharply, made a sound like ripped canvas and halted as suddenly as if it had dropped an anchor. Waverly pitched forward; the harness snapped. He hurtled across the short prow, clipping off a flagstaff bearing a triangular pink ensign, fell six feet and was skidding head over heels across the deck of the barge.

For a moment, Waverly lay half-stunned; then he staggered to his feet, holding a tattered strip of safety harness in one hand. The twifler was drifting rapidly away, some ten feet above the deck of the barge. He scrambled after it, made a despairing grab at a trailing harness strap, missed, skidded into the rail and clung there, watching the air car dwindle away downwind.

Behind him, a brilliant crimson spotlight blared into existence. Hoarse voices shouted. Other lights came up. The deck, Waverly saw, was swarming with excited figures. He ducked for the cover of a three-foot scupper, squinted as the floodlight caught him square in the face. Something hard was pressing into his hip. He groped, came out with the compact automatic he had jammed into the waistband of his pajamas. He raised the gun and fired a round into the big light. It emitted a deep-toned *whoof!*, flashed green and blue and went out.

"Hey!" a rubbery voice yelled. "I thought you boobs stuck a fresh filament in number twelve!"

"Get them extra persons in position before I put 'em over the side," another voice bassooned.

"Zero minus six mini-units and counting," a hoot came from on high.

The gobbling mob surged closer. Waverly clutched the pistol, made three yards sideways, then rose in shadow and darted toward a low deckhouse ahead. He rounded its corner, almost collided with an apparition with coarse-grained, blue wattles, two-inch eyes of a deep bottle green, a vertically hinged mouth opening on triple rows of coppery-brown fangs, all set on a snaky neck rising from a body like a baled buffalo robe shrouded in leathery wings; then he was skittering backward, making pushing motions with both hands.

"Hasrach opp irikik!" the creature boomed. "Who're youse? You scared the pants off me in that getup! Whad-dya want?"

"Izlik s-sent me," Waverly improvised.

"Oh, then you want to see the boss."

"Ah, yes, precisely. I want to see the boss."

"You want the feeding boss, the mating boss, the leisure-time boss, the honorary boss, the hereditary boss or the compulsory boss?" The monster snapped a blue cigar butt over the rail.

"The, er, boss boss!"

"Balvovats is inside, rescripting scene two. Din't you hear what happened out on the coast?"

"As a matter of fact, I just got in from Butte——"

"How did the fireball routine go?"

"Very impressive. Ah, by the way, how long before things get underway here?"

"Another five minutes."

"Thanks."

Waverly sidled past the horror, made for a lighted doorway fifty feet away. Above, invisible behind banked floodlights, someone was gabbling shrilly. Two beings appeared at the entrance as Waverly reached it. One was an armored creature mincing on six legs like a three-foot blue crab. The other appeared to be a seven-foot column of translucent yellow jelly.

"Here, you can't go in there," the crablike one barked. "*Ik urikik opsrock,* you know that!"

"Wait a minute, Sol," the gelatinous one burbled in a shaky voice like a failing tape recorder. "Can't you see he's just in from location? Look at the costume."

"A lousy job. Wouldn't fool anybody."

"What you got, Mac? Make it fast. Balvovats is ready to roll 'em."

"Ip orikip slunk," Waverly said desperately.

"Sorry, I don't savvy Glimp. Better talk local like the style boss said."

"It's the rotiple underplump!" Waverly barked. "Out of the way, before all is lost!"

"I got to have a word with Mel about his runners, which they're a little too uppity to suit me." Waverly caught the word as the two exchanged glances and moved from the doorway. He stepped through into a room dazzling with light and activity. Opposite him, a fifty-foot wall glittered with moving points of light. Before it, on high stools, half a dozen small orange-furred creatures bristling with multi-elbowed arms manipulated levers. On a raised dais to the left, a circular being with what appeared to be four heads shouted commands in all directions at once, through four megaphones.

"Okay!" Waverly heard the call. "We're all ready on one, three and four! What's the matter with two and five?"

"Here, you!" A scaled figure in a flowing pageboy bob thrust a sheaf of papers into his hand. "Take this to Blavovats; he's got holes in his head!" Waverly gaped after the donor as it turned away. The noise around him made his ears ring. Everything was rushing toward a climax at an accelerating pace, and if he didn't do something fast . . .

50

"Stop!" he yelled at the room at large. "You can't do this thing!"

"It's a heart-breaker, ain't it, kid?" a bulging being on his left chirruped in his ear. "If I would have been directing this fiasco, I'd of went for a real effect by blasting the ice caps. Now, *there's* a spectacle for you! Floods, storms——"

"Here, take these to Balvovats!" Waverly shoved the papers toward a passing creature resembling a fallen pudding. The bulgy being nictated a membrane at him, snorted, said, "Okay, okay, I'm going, ain't I?" and pushed off through the press. At a discreet distance, Waverly followed.

6

The room the impressed messenger led him to was a circular arena crowded with screens, dials, levers, flashing lights, amid a cacophony of electronic hums and buzzes, all oriented toward a central podium on which was mounted a red and white, zebra-striped swivel chair, wide enough to accommodate triplets.

"Where's Balvovats?" The unwitting guide collared a jittery organism consisting of a cluster of bristly blue legs below a striped polo shirt.

"He stepped over to Esthetic Editing for a last-minute check," a piping voice snapped. "Now leggo my shirt before I call the shop steward!"

"Give him these!" The bulbous intruder handed over the papers and departed. Waverly faded back behind the column-mounted chair, looked around hastily, put a foot on a rung——

"Two minutes," a PA voice rang. "All recorder units on station and grinding."

"Hey, you, back outside on Set Nine! You heard the two-minute call!" Waverly looked down at a foot-high composition of varicolored warts mounted on two legs like coat-hanger wire.

"Mind your tone, my man," Waverly said. "Balvovats sent me. I'm sitting in for him. Is the, er, power on?"

51

"Cripey, what a time for a OJT! Okay, sir, better get on up there. About a minute and a half to M millisecond."

Waverly clambered to the seat, slid into it, looked over an array of levers, pedals, orifices, toggle switches and paired buttons with varicolored idiot lights. "Don't monkey with the board, it's all set up," the warty one whined at his elbow. "I balanced her out personal. All you got to do is throw the load to her when you get the flash and push-field is up to full Q."

"Naturally," Waverly said. "It wouldn't do at all to push, say, this little green button here . . . ?"

"If you got to go, you should've went before you come in here. Better tighten up and wait. You only got fifty-one seconds and you're on the air."

"How about the big blue one there?"

"What for you want more light on deck? The boys are crying their eyes out now."

"This middle-sized yellow one?"

"The screens is already hot, can't you see 'em? Boy, the greenies they send out to me!"

"I know; this immense black lever is the one——"

"You don't need no filters, for Pud's sake! It's night-time!"

Waverly ran both hands through his hair and then pointed to various levers in turn: "Eenie, meenie, minie, moe . . . ."

"Lay off that one you called 'minie,' " the instructor cautioned. "You touch that, you'll dump the whole load onto the left stabilizer complex——"

A door banged. Waverly looked up. A vast, white-robed being with arms like coiled boa constrictors had burst into the room, was goggling stem-mounted eyes like peeled tomatoes at Waverly.

"Hey—come down from there, you!" the new arrival bellowed. The snaky arms whipped up toward Waverly; he ducked, seized the forbidden lever, and slammed it home.

A shudder went through the seat under him; then the floor rose up like a stricken freighter up-ending for her last dive. A loud screech sounded in Waverly's ear as the warty being bounded into his lap and wrestled with the big

52

lever. He rolled sideways, dived, saw the vast form of Balvovats cannon past and carom off the control pedestal, ophidioid members flailing murderously. Lights were flashing all around the room. A siren broke into a frantic, rising wail. Gongs gonged. Waverly, on the floor now and clinging to a cabinet support, saw an access panel pop open, exposing a foot square terminal block. "In for a penny, in for a pound," he muttered and grabbed a handful of the intricately color-coded leads and ripped them loose.

The resultant cascade of fire sent him reeling backward just as a baseball-bat-thick tentacle whipped down across the spot he had been occupying. A dull *boom!* rocked the deck plates under him. Smoke poured from the ruined circuitry. He tottered to his feet, saw Balvovats secure a grip on a stanchion and haul his bulk upright.

"You!" the giant bellowed and launched itself at Waverly. He sprang for the door, tripped, rolled aside as the door banged wide. A gaggle of frantic spectaclemakers hurtled through, collided with the irate director. On all fours, Waverly pulled himself up the slanted deck and through the door.

In the corridor, the blare of gongs and sirens was redoubled. Buffeted by milling technicians, Waverly was spun, jostled, shoved, lifted along the passage and out onto the windswept deck. All around, loose gear was sliding and bounding down the thirty-degree slant. Waverly threw himself flat, barely avoiding a ricocheting cable drum, clawed his way toward the high edge of the barge.

"There he goes!" a bull-roar sounded behind him. He twisted, saw Balvovats winching himself upward in close pursuit. One extensible member lashed out, slapped the deck bare inches short of Waverly's foot. He groped for the automatic. It was gone. Ahead, a superstructure loomed up at the barge's edge, like a miniature Eiffel Tower. He scrambled for it, got a grip on a cross-member and pulled himself around to the far side. Balvovat's questing arm grabbed after him. He held on with both hands and one foot and delivered a swift kick to the persistent member; it recoiled, as a yell sounded from the darkness below. The deck lights had failed, leaving only

53

the feeble gleam of colored rigging lights. Something struck the cross-bar by Waverly's head with a vicious *pwangg!* He clambered hastily higher.

On deck, someone had restored a spotlight to usefulnss. The smoky beam probed upward, found Waverly's feet, jumped up to pin him against a girder fifty feet above the deck.

"A fat bonus to the one that nails him!" Balvovats' furious tones roared. At once, spitting sounds broke out below, accompanied by vivid flashes of pink light. Waverly scrambled higher. The spotlight followed him. Across the deck, a door burst open and smoke and flames rushed out. Waverly felt a shock through the steel tower, saw a gout of fire erupt through curled deck plating below.

"We're sinking!" a shrill voice keened.

"Get him!" Balvovats boomed.

Waverly looked down, saw white water breaking over the base of his perch. In the glow of the navigation lights, half a dozen small creatures were swarming up the open-work in hot pursuit. Something bumped him from behind. He shied, felt another bump, reached down and felt the hard contours of the automatic, trapped in the seat of his pajamas.

"Lucky I had them cut generously," he murmured as he retrieved the weapon. Something *spangled* beside him, and a near-miss whined off into the darkness. Waverly took aim, shot out the deck light. Something plucked at his sleeve. He looked, saw torn cloth. Below, a red-eyed ball of sticky-looking fur was taking a bead on him from a distance of ten feet. He brought the automatic up and fired, fired again at a second pursuer a yard below the leader. Both assailants dropped, hit with twin splashes in the darkness below.

"Decks awash," Waverly said to himself. "*Dulce et decorum est, pro patria, et cetera.*"

Another explosion shook the stricken barge. The tower swayed. A shot whined past his face. Another struck near-by.

"Get him, troops? Get hiburbleburble . . . ." Balvovats' boom subsided. Waverly winced as a hot poker furrowed

54

his shin. He saw a flicker of movement revealed by a blue rigging light, put a round into it, saw a dark body fall with a thin bleat. The spout of fire rising from the hatch on the high edge of the deck showed a white smother of foam washed almost to the survivors clinging to the rail. A gun burped below, chipped paint by Waverly's hip. He shifted grips, leaned far out and placed a shot between a pair of overlapping, egg-white eyes. They fell away with a despairing wail.

Abruptly, the fire died with a hiss as a wave rolled entirely across the deck. Waverly felt the tower shake as a breaker thundered against it, bare yards below where he clung. The lower navigation lights gleamed up through green water now.

There was a whifling sound above. Waverly clutched his perch convulsively, looked upward.

"Fom Berj!" he yelled.

A dark ovoid shape settled down through the night toward him. He saw the cheery glow of running lights, the gleam reflected from a canopy.

"But . . . but our canopy blew away . . ." he faltered.

The twifler hove to, six feet above his head. A face like a plate of lasagna appeared over the edge. Squirmy hands, gripping an ominous-looking apparatus with a long barrel, came over the side, aimed at Waverly. A whirring sound started up. He brought up the pistol, squeezed the trigger——

There was an empty click.

"Superb!" the creature above exclaimed, extending a large grasping member over the wide to Waverly. "What an expression of primitive savagery! Great footage, my boy! Now you'd better come aboard where we can talk contract in peace!"

7

"I'm afraid I don't quite understand, Mr. Izlik," Waverly said dazedly, trying not to stare at the leathery-hided bulk draped in a Clan Stewart tartan, complete with sporran and Tam o'Shanter. "One moment I was teetering on top of a sinking tower, with a horde of furry atrocities snapping at my heels—and ten minutes later . . ." He looked wonderingly at the luxuriously appointed lounge in which he sat.

"I left my yacht anchored here at two hundred thousand feet and dropped down to spy out what Balvovats was up to," the entrepreneur explained. "I confess I wasn't above purloining a little free footage of whatever it was he was staging. Then I saw you, sir, in action, and presto! I perceived the New Wave in the moment of its creation! Of course, I secured only about three minutes' actual product. We'll have to pad it out with another hundred hours or so of the same sort of action. I can already visualize a sequence in which you find yourself pursued by flesh-eating Dinosaurs, scale a man-eating plant for safety and are attacked by flying fang-masters, make a leap across an abyss of flaming hydrocarbons and, in a single bound, attain the safety of your twifler, just as it collides with a mountaintop!"

"Ah . . . I appreciated your offer of employment," Waverly interposed, "but I'm afraid I lack the dramatic gift."

"Oh, it won't be acting," Izlik handed over a slim glass of pale fluid and seated himself across from his guest. "No, indeed! I can assure you that all my productions are recorded on location, at the actual scenes of the frightful dangers they record. I'll see to it that the perils are real enough to inspire you to the highest efforts."

"No." Waverly drained his glass and hiccupped. "I appreciate the rescue and all that, but now I really must be getting back to work——"

"What salary are you drawing now?" Izlik demanded bluntly.

"Five hundred," Waverly said.

"Ha! I'll double that! One thousand Universal Credits!"

"How much is that in dollars?"

"You mean the local exchange?" Izlik removed a note book from his sporran, writhed his features at it.

"Coconuts. . . . wampum. . . . seashells . . . green stamps . . . ah! Here we are! Dollars. One Unicred is equal to twelve hundred and sixty-five dollars and twenty-three cents." He closed the book. "A cent is a type of cow, I believe. A few are always included in local transactions to placate Vishnu, or something."

"That's . . . that's a little over a million dollars a month!"

"A minute," Izlik corrected. "You'll get more for your next picture, of course."

"I'd like to take you up on it, Mr. Izlik," Waverly said wistfully. "But I'm afraid I wouldn't survive long enough to spend it."

"As to that, if you're to play superheroes, you'll naturally require superpowers. I'll fit you out with full S-P gear. Can't have my star suffering any damage, of course."

"S-P gear?"

"Self-Preservation. Developed in my own labs at Cosmic Productions. Better than anything issued to the armed forces. Genuine poly-steel muscles, invulnerable armor, IR and UV vision, cloak of invisibility—though of course you'll use the latter only in *real* emergencies."

"It sounds——" Waverly swallowed. "Quite overwhelming," he finished.

"Wait!" a faint voice sounded from the floor. Waverly and Izlik turned to the cot where Fom Berj was struggling feebly to sit up.

"You wouldn't . . . sink so low . . . as to ally yourself . . . with these vandals . . . ." she gasped out.

"Vandals!" Izlik snorted. "I remind you, madam, it was I who took in tow your derelict twifler, which was bearing you swiftly toward a trans-Plutonian orbit!"

"Better annihilation—than help . . . from the likes of you . . ."

"I, ah, think you have an erroneous impression," Waverly put in. "Mr. Izlik here doesn't produce Galaculars. In fact, he's planning a nice, family-type entertainment that will render the planet wreckers obsolete."

"The day of the Galacular is over!" Izlik stated in positive tones. "What is a mere fractured continent, when compared with a lone hero, fighting for his life? When I

57

release my epic of the struggle of one beleaguered being, beset by a bewildering bestiary of bellicose berserkers, our fortunes will be made!"

"Oh, really?" Fom Berj listened to a brief outline of the probable impact on the theatrically minded Galactic public of the new Miniculars.

"Why, Wivery—I really think you've solved the problem!" she acknowledged at the end. "In fact—I don't suppose——" She rolled her oversized eyes at Izlik. "How about signing me on as leading lady?"

"Well—I don't know," Izlik hedged. "With a family-type audience, there might be cries of miscegenation . . . ."

"Nonsense. Take off your disguise, Wivery."

"To be perfectly candid, I'm not wearing one," Waverly replied with dignity.

"You mean——" Fom Berj stared at him. Then a titter broke from her capacious mouth. She reached up, fumbled at her throat, and with a single downward stroke, split her torso open like a banana peel. A slim arm came out and thrust the bulky costume back from round shoulders; a superb bosom emerged, followed by a piquant face with a turned-up nose topped by a cascade of carrot-red hair.

"And I thought I had to conceal my identity from *you!*" she said as she stepped from the collapsed Vorplischer suit. "And all this time you were really a Borundian!"

"A Borundian?" Waverly smiled dazedly at the graceful figure before him, modestly clad in a wisp of skintight gauze.

"Like me," Fom Berj said. "They'd never had hired me in my natural guise. We look too much like those Earth natives."

"Here," Izlik interrupted. "If you two are the same species, why is it that she's shaped like *that,* and you're not?"

"That's part of the beauty of being a, um, Borundian," Waverly said, taking the former detective's hand and looking into her smiling green eyes. "Go ahead and draw up the contracts, Mr. Izlik. You've got yourself a deal."

THE STAR-SENT KNAVES

Clyde W. Snithian was a bald eagle of a man, dark-eyed, pot-bellied, with the large, expressive hands of a rug merchant. Round-shouldered in a loose cloak, he blinked small reddish eyes at Dan Slane's travel-stained six-foot-one.

"Kelly here tells me you've been demanding to see me." He nodded toward the florid man at his side. He had a high, thin voice, like something that needed oiling. "Something about important information regarding safeguarding my paintings."

"That's right, Mr. Snithian," Dan said. "I believe I can be of great help to you."

"Help how? If you've got ideas of bilking me . . ." The reb eyes bored into Dan like hot pokers.

"Nothing like that, sir. Now, I know you have quite a system of guards here—the papers are full of it——"

"Damned busybodies! Sensation-mongers! If it wasn't for the press, I'd have no concern for my paintings today!"

"Yes sir. But my point is, the one really important spot has been left unguarded."

"Now, wait a minute——" Kelly started.

"What's that?" Snithian cut in.

"You have a hundred and fifty men guarding the house and grounds day and night——"

"Two hundred and twenty five," Kelly snapped.

"—but no one at all in the vault with the paintings," Slane finished.

"Of course not," Snithian shrilled. "Why should I post a man in the vault? It's under constant surveillance from the corridor outside."

"The Harriman paintings were removed from a locked vault," Dan said. "There was a special seal on the door. It wasn't broken."

"By the saints, he's right," Kelly exclaimed. "Maybe we ought to have a man in that vault."

"Another idiotic scheme to waste my money," Snithian snapped. "I've made you responsible for security here, Kelly! Let's have no more nonsense. And throw this nincompoop out!" Snithian turned and stalked away, his cloak flapping at his knees.

"I'll work cheap," Dan called after him as Kelly took his arm. "I'm an art lover."

"Never mind that," Kelly said, escorting Dan along the corridor. He turned in at an office and closed the door.

"Now, as the old buzzard said, I'm responsible for security here. If those pictures go, my job goes with them. Your vault idea's not bad. Just how cheap would you work?"

"A hundred dollars a week," Dan said promptly. "Plus expenses," he added.

Kelly nodded. "I'll fingerprint you and run a fast agency check. If you're clean, I'll put you on, starting tonight. But keep it quiet."

Dan looked around at the gray walls, with shelves stacked to the low ceiling with wrapped paintings. Two three-hundred-watt bulbs shed a white glare over the tile floor, a neat white refrigerator, a bunk, an armchair, a bookshelf and a small table set with paper plates, plastic utensils and a portable radio—all hastily installed at Kelly's order. Dan opened the refrigerator, looked over the stock of salami, liverwurst, cheese and beer. He opened a loaf of bread, built up a well-filled sandwich, keyed open a can of beer.

It wasn't fancy, but it would do. Phase one of the plan had gone off without a hitch.

Basically, his idea was simple. Art collections had been disappearing from closely guarded galleries and homes all over the world. It was obvious that no one could enter a locked vault, remove a stack of large canvases and leave, unnoticed by watchful guards—and leaving the locks un-damaged.

Yet the paintings were gone. Someone had been in those vaults—someone who hadn't entered in the usual way.

Theory failed at that point; that left the experimental method. The Snithian collection was the largest west of the Mississippi. With such a target, the thieves were bound to show up. If Dan sat in the vault—day and night—waiting—he would see for himself how they operated.

He finished his sandwich, went to the shelves and pulled down one of the brown-paper bundles. Loosening the string binding the package, he slid a painting into view. It was a gaily colored view of an open-air cafe, with a group of men and women in gay-ninetyish costumes gathered at a table. He seemed to remember reading something about it in a magazine. It was a cheerful scene; Dan liked it. Still, it hardly seemed worth all the effort. . .

He went to the wall switch and turned off the lights. The orange glow of the filaments died, leaving only a faint illumination from the night-light over the door. When the thieves arrived, it might give him a momentary advantage if his eyes were adjusted to the dark. He groped his way to the bunk.

So far, so good, he reflected, stretching out. When they showed up, he'd have to handle everything just right. If he scared them off there'd be no second chance. He would have lost his crack at—whatever his discovery might mean to him.

But he was ready. Let them come.

Eight hours, three sandwiches and six beers later, Dan roused suddenly from a light doze and sat up on the cot. Between him and the crowded shelving, a palely luminous framework was materializing in midair.

The apparition was an open-work cage—about the size and shape of an outhouse minus the sheathing, Dan estimated breathlessly. Two figures were visible within the structure, sitting stiffly in contoured chairs. They glowed, if anything, more brightly than the framework.

A faint sound cut into the stillness—a descending whine. The cage moved jerkily, settling toward the floor. Long blue sparks jumped, crackling, to span the closing gap; with a grate of metal, the cage settled against the floor. The spectral men reached for ghostly switches . . .

The glow died.

Dan was aware of his heart thumping painfully under his ribs. His mouth was dry. This was the moment he'd been planning for, but now that it was here——

Never mind. He took a deep breath, ran over the speeches he had prepared for the occasion:

Greeting, visitors from the Future . . .

Hopelessly corny. What about: *Welcome to the Twentieth Century* . . .

No good; it lacked spontaneity. The men were rising, their backs to Dan, stepping out of the skeletal frame. In the dim light it now looked like nothing more than a rough frame built of steel pipe, with a cluster of levers in a console before the two seats. And the thieves looked ordinary enough: Two men in gray coveralls, one slender and balding, the other shorter and round-faced. Neither of them noticed Dan, sitting rigid on the cot. The thin man placed a lantern on the table, twiddled a knob. A warm light sprang up. The visitors looked at the stacked shelves.

"Looks like the old boy's been doing all right," the shorter man said. "Fathead's gonna be pleased."

"A very gratifying consignment," his companion said. "However, we'd best hurry, Manny. How much time have we left on this charge?"

"Plenty. Fifteen minutes anyway."

The thin man opened a package, glanced at a painting.

"Ah, magnificent. Almost the equal of Picasso in his puce period."

Manny shuffled through the other pictures in the stack.

"Like always," he grumbled. "No nood dames. I like nood dames."

"Look at this, Manny! The textures alone—"

Manny looked. "Yeah, nice use of values," he conceded. "But I still prefer nood dames, Fiorello."

"And this!" Fiorello lifted the next painting. "Look at that gay play of rich browns!"

"I seen richer browns on Thirty-third Street," Manny said. "They was popular with the sparrows."

"Manny, sometimes I think your aspirations———"

"Whatta ya talkin? I use a roll-on." Manny, turning to place a painting in the cage, stopped dead as he caught sight of Dan. The painting clattered to the floor. Dan stood, cleared his throat. "Uh . . ."

"Oh-oh," Manny said. "A double-cross."

"I've—ah—been expecting you gentlemen," Dan said. "I———"

"I told you we couldn't trust no guy with nine fingers on each hand," Manny whispered hoarsely. He moved toward the cage. "Let's blow, Fiorello."

"Wait a minute," Dan said. "Before you do anything hasty———"

"Don't start nothing, Buster," Manny said cautiously. "We're plenty tough guys when aroused."

"I want to talk to you," Dan insisted. "You see, these paintings———"

"Paintings? Look, it was all a mistake. Like, we figured this was the gent's room———"

"Never mind, Manny," Fiorello cut in. "It appears there's been a leak."

Dwn shook his head. "No leak. I simply deduced———"

"Look, Fiorello," Manny said. "You chin if you want to; I'm doing a fast fade."

"Don't act hastily, Manny. You know where you'll end."

"Wait a minute!" Dan shouted. "I'd like to make a deal with you fellows."

"Ah-hah!" Kelly's voice blared from somewhere. "I knew it! Slane, you crook!"

Dan looked about wildly. The voice seemed to be issuing from a speaker. It appeared Kelly hedged his bets.

"Mr. Kelly, I can explain everything!" Dan called. He turned back to Fiorello. "Listen, I figured out———"

"Pretty clever!" Kelly's voice barked. "Inside job. But it takes more than the likes of you to outfox an old-timer like Eddie Kelly."

"Perhaps you were right, Manny," Fiorello said.

"Complications are arising. We'd best depart with all deliberate haste." He edged toward the cage.

"What about this ginzo?" Manny jerked a thumb toward Dan. "He's on to us."

"Can't be helped."

"Look—I want to go with you!" Dan shouted.

"I'll bet you do!" Kelly's voice roared. "One more minute and I'll have the door open and collar the lot of you! Came up through a tunnel, did you?"

"You can't go, my dear fellow," Fiorello said. "Room for two, no more."

Dan whirled to the cot, grabbed up the pistol Kelly had supplied. He aimed it at Manny. "You stay here, Manny! I'm going with Fiorello in the time machine."

"Are you nuts?" Manny demanded.

"I'm flattered, dear boy," Fiorello said, "but——"

"Let's get moving. Kelly will have that lock open in a minute."

"You can't leave me here!" Manny spluttered, watching Dan crowd into the cage beside Fiorello.

"We'll send for you," Dan said. "Let's go, Fiorello."

The balding man snatched suddenly for the gun. Dan wrestled with him. The pistol fell, bounced on the floor of the cage, skidded into the far corner of the vault. Manny charged, reaching for Dan as he twisted aside; Fiorello's elbow caught him in the mouth. Manny staggered back into the arms of Kelly, bursting red-faced into the vault.

"Manny!" Fiorello released his grip on Dan, lunged to aid his companion. Kelly passed Manny to one of three cops crowding in on his heels. Dan clung to the framework as Fiorello grappled with Kelly. A cop pushed past them, spotted Dan, moved in briskly for the pinch. Dan grabbed a lever at random and pulled.

Sudden silence fell as the walls of the room blowed blue. A spectral Kelly capered before the cage, fluorescing in the blue-violet. Dan swallowed hard and nudged a second lever. The cage sank like an elevator into the floor, vivid blue washing up its sides.

Hastily he reversed the control. Operating a time machine was tricky business. One little slip, and the Slane molecules would be squeezing in among brick and mortar particles . . .

But this was no time to be cautious. Things hadn't turned out just the way he'd planned, but after all, this was what he'd wanted—in a way. The time machine was his to command. And if he gave up now and crawled back into the vault, Kelly would gather him in and pin every art theft of the past decade on him.

It couldn't be *too* hard. He'd take it slowly, figure out the controls . . .

Dan took a deep breath and tried another lever. The cage rose gently, in eerie silence. It reached the ceiling and kept going. Dan gritted his teeth as an eight-inch band of luminescence passed down the cage. Then he was emerging into a spacious kitchen. A blue-haloed cook waddled to a luminous refrigerator, caught sight of Dan rising slowly from the floor, stumbled back, mouth open. The cage rose, penetrated a second ceiling. Dan looked around at a carpeted hall.

Cautiously he neutralized the control lever. The cage came to rest an inch above the floor. As far as Dan could tell, he hadn't traveled so much as a minute into the past or future.

He looked over the controls. There should be one labeled "Forward" and another labeled "Back," but all the levers were plain, unadorned black. They looked, Dan decided, like ordinary circuit-breaker type knife switches. In fact, the whole apparatus had the appearance of something thrown together hastily from common materials. Still, it worked. So far he had only found the controls for maneuvering in the usual three dimensions, but the time switch was bound to be here somewhere. . .

Dan looked up at a movement at the far end of the hall.

A girl's head and shoulders appeared, coming up a spiral staircase. In another second she would see him, and give the alarm—and Dan needed a few moments of peace and quiet in which to figure out the controls. He moved a lever. The cage drifted smoothly sideways, sliced through the wall with a flurry of vivid blue light. Dan pushed the

65

lever back. He was in a bedroom now, a wide chamber with flouncy curtains, a four-poster under a flowered canopy, a dressing table——

The door opened and the girl stepped into the room. She was young. Not over eighteen, Dan thought—as nearly as he could tell with the blue light playing around her face. She had long hair tied with a ribbon, and long legs, neatly curved. She wore shorts and carried a tennis racquet in her left hand and an apple in her right. Her back to Dan and the cage, she tossed the racquet on a table, took a bite of the apple, and began briskly unbuttoning her shirt.

Dan tried moving a lever. The cage edged toward the girl. Another; he rose gently. The girl tossed the shirt onto a chair and undid the zipper down the side of the shorts. Another lever; the cage shot toward the outer wall as the girl reached behind her back . . .

Dan blinked at the flash of blue and looked down. He was hovering twenty feet above a clipped lawn.

He looked at the levers. Wasn't it the first one in line that moved the cage ahead? He tried it, shot forward ten feet. Below, a man stepped out on the terrace, lit a cigarette, paused, started to turn his face up——

Dan jabbed at a lever. The cage shot back through the wall. He was in a plain room with a depression in the floor, a wide window with a planter filled with glowing blue plants——

The door opened. Even blue, the girl looked graceful as a deer as she took a last bite of the apple and stepped into the ten-foot-square sunken tub. Dan held his breath. The girl tossed the apple core aside, seemed to suddenly become aware of eyes on her, whirled——

With a sudden lurch that threw Dan against the steel bars, the cage shot through the wall into the open air and hurtled off with an acceleration that kept him pinned, helpless. He groped for the controls, hauled at a lever. There was no change. The cage rushed on, rising higher. In the distance, Dan saw the skyline of a town, approaching with frightful speed. A tall office building reared up fifteen stories high. He was headed dead for it.

He covered his ears, braced himself.

With an abruptness that flung him against the opposite side of the cage, the machine braked, shot through the wall and slammed to a stop. Dan sank to the floor of the cage, breathing hard. There was a loud *click!* and the glow faded.

With a lunge, Dan scrambled out of the cage. He stood looking around at a simple brown-painted office, dimly lit by sunlight filtered through elaborate venetian blinds. There were posters on the wall, a potted plant by the door, a heap of framed paintings beside it, and at the far side of the room a desk. And behind the desk—Something.

2

Dan gaped at a head the size of a beachball, mounted on a torso like a hundred-gallon bag of water. Two large brown eyes blinked at him from points eight inches apart. Immense hands with too many fingers unfolded and reached to open a brown paper carton, dip in, then toss three peanuts, deliberately, one by one, into a gaping mouth that opened just above the brown eyes.

"Who're you?" a bass voice demanded from somewhere near the floor.

"I'm . . . I'm . . . Dan Slane . . . your honor."

"What happened to Manny and Fiorello?"

"They—I—There was this cop. Kelly——"

"Oh-oh." The brown eyes blinked deliberately. The many-fingered hands closed the peanut carton and tucked it into a drawer.

"Well, it was a sweet racket while it lasted," the basso voice said. "A pity to terminate so happy an enterprise. Still . . ." A noise like an amplified bronx cheer issued from the wide mouth.

"How . . . what . . . ?"

"The carrier returns here automatically when the charge drops below a critical value," the voice said. "A necessary measure to discourage big ideas on the part of wisenheimers in my employ. May I ask how you happen to be aboard the carrier, by the way?"

67

"I just wanted—I mean, after I figured out—that is, the police . . . I went for help," Dan finished lamely.

"Help? Out of the picture, unfortunately. One must maintain one's anonymity, you'll appreciate. My operation here is under wraps at present. Ah, I don't suppose you brought any paintings?"

Dan shook his head. He was staring at the posters. His eyes, accustoming themselves to the gloom of the office, could now make out the vividly drawn outline of a creature resembling an alligator-headed giraffe rearing up above scarlet foliage. The next poster showed a face similar to the beachball behind the desk, with red circles painted around the eyes. The next was a view of a yellow volcano spouting fire into a black sky.

"Too bad." The words seemed to come from under the desk. Dan squinted, caught a glimpse of coiled purplish tentacles. He gulped and looked up to catch a brown eye upon him. Only one. The other seemed to be busily at work studying the ceiling.

"I hope," the voice said, "that you ain't harboring no reactionary racial prejudices."

"Gosh, no," Dan reassured the eye. "I'm crazy about—uh——"

"Vorplischers," the voice said. "From Vorplisch, or Vega, as you call it." The Bronx cheer sounded again. "How I long to glimpse once more my native fens! Wherever one wanders, there's no pad like home."

"That reminds me," Dan said. "I have to be running along now." He sidled toward the door.

"Stick around, Dan," the voice rumbled. "How about a drink? I can offer you Chateau Neuf du Pape, '59, romance Conte, '32, goat's milk, Pepsi——"

"No, thanks."

"If you don't mind, I believe I'll have a Big Orange." The Vorplischer swiveled to a small refrigerator, removed an immense bottle fitted with a nipple and turned back to Dan. "Now, I got a proposition which may be of some interest to you. The loss of Manny and Fiorello is a serious blow, but we may yet recoup the situation. You made the scene at a most opportune time. What I got in mind is,

68

with those two clowns out of the picture, a vacancy exists on my staff, which you might well fill. How does that grab you?"

"You mean you want me to take over operating the time machine?"

"Time machine?" The brown eyes blinked alternately. "I fear some confusion exists. I don't quite dig the significance of the term."

"That thing," Dan jabbed a thumb toward the cage. "The machine I came here in. You want me——"

"Time machine," the voice repeated. "Some sort of chronometer, perhaps?"

"Huh?"

"I pride myself on my command of the local idiom, yet I confess the implied concept snows me." The nine-fingered hands folded on the desk. The beachball head leaned forward interestedly. "Clue me, Dan. What's a time machine?"

"Well, it's what you use to travel through time."

The brown eyes blinked in agitated alternation. "Apparently I've loused up my investigation of the local cultural background. I had no idea you were capable of that sort of thing." The immense head leaned back, the wide mouth opening and closing rapidly. "And to think I've been spinning my wheels collecting primitive 2-D art!"

"But—don't you have a time machine? I mean, isn't that one?"

"That? That's merely a carrier. Now tell me more about your time machines. A fascinating concept! My superiors will be delighted at this development—and astonished as well. They regard this planet as Endsville."

"Your superiors?" Dan eyed the window; much too far to jump. Maybe he could reach the machine and try a getaway.

"I hope you're not thinking of leaving suddenly," the beachball said, following Dan's glance. One of the eighteen fingers touched a six-inch yellow cylinder lying on the desk. "Until the carrier is fueled, I'm afraid it's quite useless. But, to put you in the picture, I'd best introduce myself and explain my mission here. I'm Blote, Trader

Fourth Class, in the employ of the Vegan Confederation. My job is to devlop new sources of novelty items for the impulse-emporiums of the entire Secondary Quadrant."

"But the way Manny and Fiorello came sailing in through the wall! That *has* to be a time machine they were riding in. Nothing else could just materialize out of thin air like that."

"You seem to have a time-machine fixation, Dan," Blote said. "You shouldn't assume, just because you people have developed time travel, that everyone has. Now——" Blote's voice sank to a bass whisper—"I'll make a deal with you, Dan. You'll secure a small time machine in good condition for me. And in return——"

"*I'm* supposed to supply *you* with a time machine?"

Bote waggled a stubby forefinger at Dan. "I dislike pointing it out, Dan, but you are in a rather awkward position at the moment. Illegal entry, illegal possession of property, trespass—then doubtless some embarrassment exists back at the Snithian residence. I daresay Mr. Kelly would have a warm welcome for you. And, of course, I myself would deal rather harshly with any attempt on your part to take a powder." The Vegan flexed all eighteen fingers, drummed his tentacles under the desk, and rolled one eye, bugging the other at Dan.

"Whereas, on the other hand," Blote's bass voice went on, "you and me got the basis of a sweet deal. You supply the machine, and I fix you up with an abundance of the local medium of exchange. Equitable enough, I should say. What about it, Dan?"

"Ah, let me see," Dan temporized. "Time machine. Time machine——"

"Don't attempt to weasel on me, Dan," Blote rumbled ominously.

"I'd better look in the phone book," Dan suggested.

Silently, Blote produced a dog-eared directory. Dan opened it.

"Time, time. Let's see . . ." He brightened. "Time, Incorporated; local branch office. Two twenty-one Maple Street."

70

"A sales center?" Blote inquired. "Or a manufacturing complex?"

"Both," Dan said. "I'll just nip over and——"

"That won't be necessary, Dan," Blote said. "I'll accompany you." He took the directory, studied it.

"Remarkable! A common commodity, openly on sale, and I failed to notice it. Still, a ripe nut can fall from a small tree as well as from a large." He went to his desk, rummaged, came up with a handful of fuel cells. "Now, off to gather in the time machine." He took his place in the carrier, patted the seat beside him with a wide hand. "Come, Dan. Get a wiggle on."

Hesitantly, Dan moved to the carrier. The bluff was all right up to a point—but the point had just about been reached. He took his seat. Blote moved a lever. The familiar blue glow sprang up. "Kindly direct me, Dan," Blote demanded. "Two twenty-one Maple Street, I believe you said."

"I don't know the town very well," Dan said, "but. Maple's over that way."

Blote worked levers. The carrier shot out into a ghostly afternoon sky. Faint outlines of buildings, like faded negatives, spread below. Dan looked around, spotted lettering on a square five-story structure.

"Over there," he said. Blote directed the machine as it swooped smoothly toward the flat roof Dan indicated.

"Better let me take over now," Dan suggested. "I want to be sure to get us to the right place."

"Very well, Dan."

Dan dropped the carrier through the roof, passed down through a dimly seen office. Blote twiddled a small knob. The scene around the cage grew even fainter. "Best we remain unnoticed," he explained.

The cage descended steadily. Dan peered out, searching for identifying landmarks. He leveled off at the second floor, cruised along a barely visible corridor. Blote's eyes rolled, studying the small chambers along both sides of the passage at once.

"Ah, this must be the assembly area" he exclaimed. "I

see the machines employ a bar-type construction, not unlike our carriers."

"That's right," Dan said, staring through the haziness. "This is where they do time . . ." He tugged at a lever suddenly; the machine veered left, flickered through a barred door, came to a halt. Two nebulous figures loomed beside the cage. Dan cut the switch. If he'd guessed wrong——

The scene flouresced, sparks crackling, then popped into sharp focus. Blote scrambled out, brown eyes swiveling to take in the concrete walls, the barred door and——

"You!" a hoarse voice bellowed.

"Grab him!" someone yelled.

Blote recoiled, threshing his ambulatory members in a fruitless attempt to regain the carrier as Manny and Fiorello closed in. Dan hauled at a lever. He caught a last glimpse of three struggling, blue-lit figures as the carrier shot away through the cell wall.

3

Dan slumped back against the seat with a sigh. Now that he was in the clear, he would have to decide on his next move—fast. There was no telling what other resources Blote might have. He would have to hide the carrier, then——

A low growling was coming from somewhere, rising in pitch and volume. Dan sat up, alarmed. This was no time for a malfunction.

The sound rose higher, into a penetrating wail. There was no sign of mechanical trouble. The carrier glided on, swooping now over a nebulous landscape of trees and houses. Dan covered his ears again the deafening shriek, like all the police sirens in town blaring at once. If the carrier stopped it would be a long fall from here. Dan worked the controls, dropping toward the distant earth.

The noise semed to lessen, descending the scale. Dan slowed, brought the carrier in to the corner of a wide park. He dropped the last few inches and cut the switch.

As the glow died, the siren faded into silence.

Dan stepped from the carrier looked around. Whatever

he noise was, it hadn't attracted any attention from the scattered pedestrians in the park. Perhaps it was some sort of burglar alarm. But if so, why hadn't it gone into action earlier? Dan took a deep breath. Sound or no sound, he would have to get back into the carrier and transfer it to a secluded spot where he could study it at leisure. He stepped back in, reached for the controls——

There was a sudden chill in the air. The bright surface of the dials before him frosted over. There was a loud *pop!* like a flashbulb exploding. Dan stared from the seat at an iridescent rectangle which hung suspended near the carrier. Its surface rippled, faded to blackness. In a swirl of frosty air, a tall figure dressed in a tight-fitting white uniform stepped through.

Dan gaped at the small rounded head, the dark-skinned long-nosed face, the long, muscular arms, the hands, their backs tufted with curly red-brown hair, the strange long-heeled feet in soft boots. A neat pillbox cap with a short visor was strapped low over the deep-set yellowish eyes, which turned in his direction. The wide mouth opened in a smile which showed square yellowish teeth.

"*Alors, Monsieur,*" the newcomer said, bending his knees and back in a quick bow. "*Vous êtes une indigine, n'est ce pas?*"

"No compree," Dan choked out. "Uh . . . juh no parlay Fransay . . ."

"My error. This is the Anglic colonial sector, isn't it? Stupid of me. Permit me to introduce myself. I'm Dzhackoon, Field Agent of Class Five, Interdimensional Monitor Service."

"That siren," Dan said. "Was that you?"

Dzhackoon nodded. "For a moment, it appeared you were disinclined to stop. I'm glad you decided to be reasonable."

"What outfit did you say you were with?" Dan asked.

"The Interdimensional Monitor Service."

"Inter-what?"

"Dimensional. The word is imprecise, of course, but it's the best our language coder can do, using the Anglic vocabulary."

73

"What do you want with me?"

Dzhackoon smiling reprovingly. "You know the penalty for operation of an unauthorized reversed-phase vehicle in Interdicted territory. I'm afraid you'll have to come along with me to Headquarters."

"Wait a minute! You mean you're arresting me?"

"That's a harsh term, but I suppose it amounts to that."

"Look here, uh—Dzhackoon. I just wandered in off the street. I don't know anything about Interdicts and re-versed-whozis vehicles. Just let me out of here."

Dzhackoon shook his head. "I'm afraid you'll have to tell it to the Inspector." He smiled amiably, gestured toward the shimmering rectangle through which he had ar-rived. From the edge, it was completely invisible. It looked, Dan thought, like a hole snipped in reality. He glanced at Dzhackoon. If he stepped in fast and threw a left to the head and followed up with a right to the short ribs——

"I'm armed, of course," the Agent said apologetically.

"Okay," Dan sighed. "But I'm going under protest."

"Don't be nervous," Dzhackoon said cheerfully. "Just step through quickly."

Dan edged up to the glimmering surface. He gritted his teeth, closed his eyes and took a step. There was a mo-mentary sensation of searing heat . . .

His eyes flew open. He was in a long, narrow room with walls finished in bright green tile. Hot yellow light flooded down from the high ceiling. Along the wall, a series of cubicles were arranged. Tall, white-uniformed creatures moved briskly about. Nearby stood a group of short, im-mensely burly individuals in yellow. Lounging against the wall at the far end of the room, Dan glimpsed a round-shouldered figure in red, with great bushes of hair fringing a bright blue face. An arm even longer than Dzhackoon's wielded a toothpick on a row of great white fangs.

"This way," Dzhackoon said. Dan followed him to a cubicle, curious eyes following him. A creature indis-tinguishable from the Field Agent except for a twist of red braid on each wrist looked up from a desk.

"I've picked up that reversed-phase violator, Ghunt,"

74

Dzhackoon said. "Anglic Sector, Locus C 922A4."

Ghunt rose. "Let me see; Anglic Sector . . . Oh, yes." He extemded a hand. Dan took it gingerly; it was a strange hand—hot, dry and coarse-skinned, like a dog's paw. He pumped it twice and let it go.

"Wonderfully expressive," Ghunt said. "Empty hand, no weapon. The implied savagery . . ." He eyed Dan curiously.

"Remarkable. I've studied your branch, of course, but I've never had the pleasure of actually seeing one of you chaps before. That skin; amazing. Ah . . . may I look a your hands?"

Dan extended a hand. The other took it in bony fingers, studied it, turned it over, examined the nails. Stepping closer, he peered at Dan's eyes and hair.

"Would you mind opening your mouth, please?" Dan complied. Ghunt clucked, eyeing the teeth. He walked around Dan, murmuring his wonderment.

"Uh . . . pardon my asking," Dan said, "but are you what—uh—people are going to look like in the future?"

"Eh?" The round yellowish eyes blinked; the wide mouth curved in a grin. "I doubt that very much, old chap." He chuckled. "Can't undo half a million years of divergent evolution, you know."

"You mean you're from the past?" Dan croaked.

"The past? I'm afraid I don't follow you."

"You don't mean—we're all going to die out and monkeys are going to take over?" Dan blurted.

"Monkeys? Let me see. I've heard of them. Some sort of small primate, like a miniature Anthropos. You have them at home, do you? Fascinating!" He shook his head regretfully. "I certainly wish regulations allowed me to pay your sector a visit."

"But you *are* time travelers," Dan insisted.

"Time travelers?" Ghunt laughed aloud.

"An exploded theory," Dzhackoon said. "Superstition."

"Then how did you get to the park from here?"

"A simple focused portal. Merely a matter of elementary stressed-field mechanics."

"That doesn't tell me much," Dan said. "Where am I? Who are you?"

"Explanations are in order, of course," Ghunt said. "Have a chair. Now, if I remember correctly, in your locus, there are only a few species of Anthropos extant——"

"Just the one," Dzhackoon put in. "These fellows look fragile, but oh, brother!"

"Oh, yes, I recall. This was the locus where the hairless variant systematically hunted down other varieties." He clucked at Dan reprovingly. "Don't you find it lonely?"

"Of course, there are a couple of rather curious retarded forms there," Dzhackoon said. "Actual living fossils; subintellectual Anthropos. There's one called the gorilla, and the chimpanzee, the orang-utan, the gibbon—and, of course, a whole spectrum of the miniature forms."

"I suppose that when the ferocious mutation established its supremacy, the others retreated to the less competitive ecological niches and expanded at that level," Ghunt mused. "Pity. I assume the gorilla and the others are degenerate forms?"

"Possibly."

"Excuse me," Dan said. "But about that explanation . . ."

"Oh, sorry. Well, to begin with Dzhackoon and I are—ah—Australopithecines, I believe your term is. We're one of the many varieties of Anthropos native to normal loci. The workers in yellow, whom you may have noticed, are akin to your extinct Neanderthals. Then there are the Pekin derivatives—the blue-faced chaps—and the Rhodesians——"

"What are these loci you keep talking about? And how can cave men still be alive?"

Ghunt's eyes wandered past Dan. He jumped to his feet. "Ah, good day, Inspector!" Dan turned. A grizzled Australopithecine with a tangle of red braid at collar and wrists stared at him glumly.

"Harrumph!" the Inspector said. "Albinism and alopecia. Not catching, I hope?"

76

"A genetic deficiency, excellency," Dzhackoon said. "This is a Homo Sapiens, a naturally bald form from a rather curious locus."

"Sapiens? Sapiens? Now, that seems to ring a bell." The oldster blinked at Dan. "You're not——" He waggled fingers in instinctive digital-mnemonic stimulus. Abruptly he stiffened. "Why, this is one of those fratricidal deviants!" He backed off. "He should be under restraint, Ghunt! Constable! Get a strong-arm squad in here! This creature is dangerous!"

"Inspector, I'm sure——" Ghunt started.

"That's an order!" the Inspector barked. He switched to an incomprehensible language, bellowed more commands. Several of the thickset Neanderthal types appeared, moving in to seize Dan's arms. He looked around at chinless, wide-mouthed brown faces with incongruous blue eyes and lank blond hair.

"What's this all about?" he demanded. "I want a lawyer!"

"Never mind that!" the Inspector shouted. "I know how to deal with miscreants of your stripe!" He stared distastefully at Dan. "Hairless! Putty-colored! Revolting! Planning more mayhem, are you? Preparing to branch out into the civilized loci to wipe out all competitive life, is that it?"

"I brought him here, Inspector," Dzhackoon put in. "It was a routine traffic violation."

"I'll decide what's routine here! Now, Sapiens! What fiendish scheme have you up your sleeve, eh?"

"Daniel Slane, civilian, Social Security number 456-7329-988," Dan said.

"Eh?"

"Name, rank and serial number," Dan explained. "I'm not answering any other questions."

"This means penal relocation, Sapiens! Unlawful departure from native locus, willful obstruction of justice——"

"You forgot being born without permission and unauthorized breathing."

"Insolence!" the Inspector snarled. "I'm warning you,

77

Sapiens, it's in my power to make things miserable for you. Now, how did you induce Agent Dzhackoon to bring you here?"

"Well, a good fairy came and gave me three wishes———"

"Take him away," the Inspector screeched. "Sector 97, an unoccupied locus."

"Unoccupied? That seems pretty extreme, doesn't it?" one of the guards commented, wrinkling his heavily ridged brow.

"Unoccupied! If it bothers you, perhaps I can arrange for you to join him there!"

The Neanderthaloid guard yawned widely, showing white teeth. He nodded to Dan, motioned him ahead. "Don't mind Spoghodo," he said loudly. "He's getting old."

"Sorry about all this," a voice hissed near Dan's ear. Dzhackoon—or Ghunt, he couldn't say which—leaned near. "I'm afraid you'll have to go along to the penal area, but I'll try to straighten things out later."

Back in the concouse, Dan's guard escorted him past cubicles where busy IDMS agents reported to harassed seniors, through an archway into a room lined with narrow gray panels. It looked like a gym locker room.

"Ninety-seven," the guard said. He went to a wall chart, studied the fine print with the aid of a blunt, hair finger, then set a dial on the wall. "Here we go," he said. He pushed a button beside one of the lockers. Its surface clouded and became iridescent.

"Just step through fast. Happy landings."

"Thanks." Dan ducked his head and pushed through the opening in a puff of frost.

He was standing on a steep hillside, looking down across a sweep of meadow to a plain far below. There were clumps of trees, and a river. In the distance a herd of animals grazed among low shrubbery. No road wound along the valley floor; no boats dotted the river; no village nestled at its bend. The far hills were innocent of trails, fences, houses, the rectangles of plowed acres. There were no contrails in the wide blue sky. No vagrant aroma of exhaust fumes, no mutter of internal combustion, no tin cans, no pop bottles——

In short, no people.

Dan turned. The Portal still shimmered faintly in the bright air. He thrust his head through, found himself staring into the locker room. The yellow-clad Neanderthaloid glanced at him.

"Say," Dan said, ignoring the sensation of a hot wire around his neck, "can't we talk this thing over?"

"Better get your head out of there before it shuts down," the guard said cheerfully. "Otherwise—ssskkkttt!"

"What about some reading matter? And look, I get these head colds. Does the temperature drop here at night? Any dangerous animals? What do I eat?"

"Here," the guard reached into a hopper, took out a handful of pamphlets. "These are supposed to be for guys that are relocated without prejudice. You know, poor slobs that just happened to see too much; but I'll let you have one. Let's see . . . Anglic, Anglic . . ." He selected one, handed it to Dan.

"Thanks."

"Better get clear."

Dan withdrew his head. He sat down on the grass and looked over the booklet. It was handsomely printed in gay colors. WELCOME TO RELOCATION CENTER NO. 23 said the cover. Below the heading was a photo of a group of sullen-looking creatures of varying heights and degrees of hairiness wearing paper hats. The caption read: *Newcomers Are Welcomed Into a Gay Round of Social Activity. Hi, Newcomer!*

Dan opened the book. A photo showed a scene identical to the one before him, except that in place of the meadow, there was a parklike expanse of lawn, dotted with rambling buildings with long porches lined with rockers. There were picnic tables under spreading trees, and beyond, on the river, a yacht basin crowded with canoes and rowboats.

"Life in a Community Center is Grand Fun!" Dan read.

"Activities! Brownies, Cub Scouts, Boy Scouts, Girl Scouts, Sea Scouts, Tree Scouts, Cave Scouts, PTA, Shriners, Bear Cult, Rotary, Daughters of the Eastern Star, Mothers of the Big Banana, Dianetics—you name it! A Group for Everyone, and Everyone in a Group!

Classes in conversational Urdu, Sprotch, Yiddish, Gaelic, Fundu, etc; knot-tying, rug-hooking, leather-work, Greek Dancing, fingerpainting and many, many others!

Little Theatre!

Indian Dance Pageants!

Round Table Discussions!

Town Meetings!

Dan thumbed on through the pages of emphatic print, stopped at a double-page spread labeled, *A Few Do's and Don'ts.*

* All of us want to make a GO of relocation. So—let's remember the Uranium Rule: Don't Do It! The Other Guy May be Bigger!

* Remember the Other Fellow's Taboos!

What to you might be merely a wholesome picnic or mating bee may offend others. What some are used to doing in groups, others consider a solitary activity. Most taboos have to do with eating, sex, elimination or gods; so remember look before you sit down, lie down, squat down or kneel down!

* Ladies With Beards Please Note:

Friend husband may be on the crew clearing clogged drains—so watch that shedding in the lavatories, eh, girls? And you fellas, too! Sure, good grooming pays—but groom each other out in the open, okay?

* NOTE, There has been some agitation for separate but equal facilities. Now, honestly, folks, is that in the spirit of Center No. 23? Males and females *will continue to use the same johns* as always. No sexual chauvinism will be tolerated.

* A Word to the Kiddies!

No brachiating will be permitted in the Social Center area. After all, a lot of the Dads sleep up there. There are plentyof other trees!

* Daintiness Pays!

In these more-active-than-ever days, Personal Effluvium can get away from us almost before we notice. And that hearty scent may not be as satisfying to others as it is to ourselves! So remember, fellas, watch that P. E.! (Lye soap, eau de Cologne, flea powder and other beaty aids available at supply shed!)

Dan tossed the book aside. There were worse things than solitude. It looked like a pretty nice world—and it was all his.

The entire North American continent, all of South America, Europe, Asia, Africa—the works. He could cut down trees, build a hut, furnish it. There'd be hunting—he could make a bow and arrows—and the skins would do to make clothes. He could start a little farming, fish the streams, sun bathe—all the things he'd never had time to do back home. It wouldn't be so bad. And eventually Dzhackoon would arrange for his release. It might be just the kind of vacation——

"Ah Dan, my boy!" a bass voice boomed. Dan jumped and spun around.

Blote's immense face blinked at him from the Portal. There was a large green bruise over one eye. He wagged a finger reproachfully.

"That was a dirty trick, Dan. My former employees were somewhat disgruntled, I'm sorry to say. But we'd best be off now. There's no time to waste."

"How did you get here?" Dan demanded.

"I employed a pocket signaler to recall my carrier—and none too soon." He touched his bruised eye gingerly. "A glance at the instruments showed me that you had visited the park. I followed and observed a TDMS Portal. Being of an adventurous turn and, of course, concerned for your welfare, I stepped through——"

81

"Why didn't they arrest you? I was picked up for operating the carrier."

"They had some such notion. A whiff of stun gas served to discourage them. Now let's hurry along before the management revives."

"Wait a minute, Blote. I'm not sure I want to be rescued by you—in spite of your concern for my welfare."

"Rubbish, Dan! Come along." Blote looked around. "Frightful place! No population! No commerce! No deals!"

"It has its compensations. I think I'll stay. You run along."

"Abandon a colleague? Never!"

"If you're still expecting me to deliver a time machine, you're out of luck. I don't have one."

"No? Ah, well, in a way I'm relieved. Such a device would upset accepted physical theory. Now, Dan, you mustn't imagine I harbor ulterior motives—but I believe our association will yet prove fruitful."

Dan rubbed a finger across his lower lip thoughtfully. "Look, Blote, you need my help. Maybe you can help me at the same time. If I come along, I want it understood that we work together. I have an idea——"

"But of course, Dan! Now shake a leg!"

Dan sighed and stepped through the portal. The yellow-clad guard lay on the floor, snoring. Blote led the way back into the great hall. TDMS officials were scattered across the floor, slumped over desks or lying limp in chairs. Blote stopped before one of a row of shimmering portals.

"After you, Dan."

"Are you sure this is the right one?"

"Quite."

Dan stepped through in the now familiar chill and found himself back in the park. A small dog sniffing at the carrier caught sight of Blote, lowered his leg and fled.

"I want to pay Mr. Snithian a visit," Dan said, climbing into a seat.

"My idea exactly," Blote ageed, lowering his bulk into place.

"Don't get the idea I'm going to help you steal anything."

"Dan! A most unkind remark. I merely wish to look into certain matters."

"Just so you don't start looking into the safe."

Blote tsked, moved a lever. The carrier climbed over a row of blue trees and headed west.

4

Blote brought the carrier in high over the Snithian estate, dropped lower and descended gently through the roof. The pale, spectral servants moving about their duties in the upper hall failed to notice the wraithlike cage passing soundlessly among them.

In the dining room, Dan caught sight of the girl—Snithian's daughter, perhaps—arranging shadowy flowers on a sideboard.

"Let me take it," Dan whispered. Blote nodded. Dan steered for the kitchen, guided the carrier to the spot on which he had first emerged from the vault, then edged down through the floor. He brought the carrier to rest and neutralized all switches in a shower of sparks and blue light.

The vault door stood open. There were pictures stacked on the bunk now, against the wall, on the floor. Dan stepped from the carrier, went to the nearest heap of paintings. They had been dumped hastily, it seemed. They weren't even wrapped. He examined the topmost canvas, still in a heavy frame; as though, he reflected, it had just been removed from a gallery wall——

"Let's look around for Snithian," Dan said. "I want to talk to him."

"I suggest we investigate the upper floors, Dan. Doubtless his personal pad is there."

"You use the carrier; I'll go up and look the house over."

"As you wish, Dan." Blote and the carrier flickered and faded from view.

Dan stooped, picked up the pistol he had dropped in the

83

scuffle with Fiorello and stepped out ino the hall. All was silent. He climbed stairs, looked into rooms. The house seemed deserted. On the third floor he went along a corridor, checking each room. The last room on the west side was fitted as a study. There was a stack of paintings on a table near the door. Dan went to them, examined the top one.

It looked familiar. Wasn't it one that *Look* said was in the Art Institute at Chicago?

There was creak as of an unoiled hinge. Dan spun around. A door stood open at the far side of the room—a connecting door to a bedroom, probably.

"Keep well away from the carrier, Mr. Slane," a high thin voice said from the shadows. The tall, cloaked figure of W. Clyde Snithian stepped into view, a needle-barreled pistol in his hand.

"I thought you'd be back," he piped. "It makes my problem much simpler. If you hadn't appeared soon it would have been necessary for me to shift the scene of my operations. That would have been a nuisance."

Dan eyed the gun. "There are a lot more paintings downstairs than there were when I left," he said. "I don't know much about art, but I recognize a few of them."

"Copies," Snithian snapped.

"This is no copy," Dan tapped the top painting on the stack. "It's an original. You can feel the brushwork."

"Not prints, of course. Copies." Snithian whinnied. "Exact copies."

"These paintings are stolen, Mr. Snithian. Why would a wealthy man like you take to stealing art?"

"I'm not here to answer questions, Mr. Slane!" The weapon in Snithian's hand bugged. A wave of pain swept over Dan. Snithian cackled, lowering the gun. "You'll soon learn better manners."

Dan's hand went to his pocket, came out holding the automatic. He aimed it at Snithian's face. The industrialist froze, eyes on Dan's gun.

"Drop the gun." Snithian's weapon clattered to the floor. "Now let's go and find Kelly."

84

"Wait!" Snithian shrilled. "I can make you a rich man, Slane."

"Not by stealing paintings."

"You don't understand. This is more than petty larceny!"

"That's right. It's grand larceny. These pictures are worth thousands."

"I can show you things that will completely change your attitude. Actually, I've acted throughout in the best interests of humanity!"

Dan gestured with the gun. "Don't plan anything clever. I'm not used to guns. This thing will go off at the least excuse, and then I'd have a murder to explain."

"That would be an inexcusable blunder on your part!" Snithian keened. "I'm a very important figure, Slane." He crossed the deep-pile rug to a glass-doored cabinet. "This," he said, taking out a flat black box, "contains a fortune in precious stones." He lifted the lid. Dan stepped closer. A row of brilliant gems nestled in a bed of cotton.

"Rubies?"

"Flawless—and perfectly matched." Snithian whinnied. "*Perfectly* matched. Worth a fortune. They're yours, if you cooperate."

"You said you were going to change my attitude. Better get started."

"Listen to me, Slane. I'm not operating independently. I'm employed by the Ivroy whose power is incalculable. My assignment has been to rescue from destruction irreplacable works of art fated to be consumed in atomic fire."

"What do you mean—fated?"

"The Ivroy knows these things. These paintings—all your art—are unique in the galaxy. Others admire but they cannot emulate. In the cosmos of the far future, the few surviving treasures of dawn art will be valued beyond all other wealth. They alone will give a renewed glimpse of the universe as it appeared to the eyes of your strange race in its glory."

85

"My strange race?"

Snithian drew himself up. "I am not of your race." He threw his cloak aside and straightened.

Dan gasped as Snithian's body unfolded, rising up, long, three-jointed arms flexing, stretching out. The bald head ducked now under the beamed ceiling. Snithian chuckled shrilly.

"What about that inflexible attitude of yours, now, Mr. Slane?" he piped. "Have I made my point?"

"Yes, but——" Dan squeaked. He cleared his throat and tried again. "But I've still got the gun."

"Oh, that." An eight-foot arm snaked out, flicked the gun aside. "I've only temporized with you because you can be useful to me, Mr. Slane. I dislike running about, and I therefore employ locals to do my running for me. Accept my offer of employment, and you'll be richly rewarded."

"Why me?"

"You already know of my presence here. If I can enlist your loyalty, there will be no need to dispose of you with the attendant annoyance from police, relatives and busybodies. I'd like you to act as my agent in the collection of the works."

"Nuts to you!" Dan said. "I'm not helping any bunch of skinheads commit robbery."

"This is for the Ivroy, you fool!" Snithian said. "The mightiest power in the cosmos!"

"This Ivroy doesn't sound so hot to me—robbing art galleries——"

"To be adult is to be disillusioned. Only realities count. But no matter. The question remains: Will you serve me loyally?"

"Hell, no!" Dan snapped.

"Too bad. I see you mean what you say. It's to be expected, I suppose. Even an infant fire-cat has fangs."

"You're damn right I mean it. How did you get Manny and Fiorello on your payroll? I'm surprised even a couple of bums would go to work for a scavenger like you."

"I suppose you refer to the precious pair recruited by Blote. That was a mistake, I fear. It seemed perfectly reasonable at the time. Tell me, how did you overcome the

86

Vegan? They're a very capable race, generally speaking."

"You and he work together, eh?" Dan said. "That makes things a little clearer. This is the collection station and Blote is the fence."

"Enough of your conjectures. You leave me no choice but to dispose of you. It's a nuisance, but it can't be helped. I'm afraid I'll have to ask you to accompany me down to the vault."

Dan eyed the door; if he were going to make a break, now was the time——

The whine of the carrier sounded. The ghostly cage glided through the wall and settled gently between Dan and Snithian. The glow died.

Blote waved cheerfully to Dan as he eased his grotesque bulk from the seat.

"Good day to you, Snithian," Blote boomed. "I see you've met Dan. An enterprising fellow."

"What brings you here, Gom Bloke?" Snithian shrilled. "I thought you'd be well on your way to Vorplisch by now."

"I was tempted, Snithian. But I don't spook easy. There is the matter of some unfinished business."

"Excellent!" Snithian exclaimed. "I'll have another consignment ready for you by tomorrow."

"Tomorrow! How is it possible, with Manny and Fiorello lodged in the hoosegow?" Blote looked around; his eye fell on the stacked paintings. He moved across to them, lifted one, glanced at the next, then shuffled rapidly through the stack. He turned.

"What duplicity is this, Snithian!" he rumbled. "All identical! Our agreement called for limited editions, not mass production! My principals will be furious! My reputation——"

"Shrivel your reputation!" Snithian keened. "I have more serious problems at the moment! My entire position's been compromised. I'm faced with the necessity for disposing of this blundering fool!"

"Dan? Why, I'm afraid I can't allow that, Snithian." Blote moved to the carrier, dumped an armful of duplicate paintings in the cage. "Evidence," he said. "The confederation has methods for dealing with sharp practice. Come, Dan, if you're ready . . ."

"You dare to cross me?" Snithian hissed. "I, who act for the Ivroy?"

Blote motioned to the carrier. "Get in, Dan. We'll be going now." He rolled both eyes to bear on Snithian. "And I'll deal with you later," he rumbled. "No one pulls a fast one on Gom Bloke, Trader Fourth Class—or on the Vegan Federation."

Snithian moved suddenly, flicking out a spidery arm to seize the weapon he had dropped, aim and trigger. Dan, in a wash of pain, felt his knees fold. He fell slackly to the floor. Beside him, Blote sagged, his tentacles limp.

"I credited you with more intelligence," Snithian cackled. "Now I have an extra ton of protoplasm to dispose of. The carrier will be useful in that connection."

5

Dan felt a familiar chill in the air. A Portal appeared. In a puff of icy mist, a tall figure stepped through.

Gone was the tight uniform. In its place, the lanky Australopithecine wore skin-tight blue-jeans and a loose sweat shirt. An oversized beret clung to the small round head. Immense dark glasses covered the yellowish eyes, and sandals flapped on the bare, long-toed feet. Dzhackoon waved a long cigarette holder at the group.

"Ah, a stroke of luck! How nice to find you standing by. I had expected to have to conduct an intensive search within the locus. Thus the native dress. However——" Dzhackoon's eyes fell on Snithian standing stiffly by, the gun out of sight.

"You're of a race unfamiliar to me," he said. "Still, I assume you're aware of the Interdicton all Anthropoid populated loci?"

"And who might you be?" Snithian inquired loftily.

"I'm a Field Agent of the Interdimensional Monitor Service."

"Ah, yes. Well, your Interdict means nothing to me. I'm operating directly under Ivroy auspices." Snithian touched a glittering pin on his drab cloak.

Dzhackoon sighed. "There goes the old arrest record."

"He's a crook!" Dan cut in. "He's been robbing art galleries!"

"Keep calm, Dan," Blote murmured. "No need to be overly explicit."

The Agent turned to look the Trader over.

"Vegan, aren't you? I imagine you're the fellow I've been chasing."

"Who, me?" the bass voice rumbled. "Look, officer, I'm a home-loving family man, just passing through. As a matter of fact——"

The uniformed creature nodded toward the paintings in the carrier. "Gathered a few souvenirs, I see."

"For the wives and kiddy. Just a little something to brighten up the hive."

"The penalty for exploitation of a subcultural anthropoid-occupied body is stasis for a period not to exceed one reproductive cycle. If I recall my Vegan biology, that's quite a period."

"Why, officer! Surely you're not putting the arm on a respectable law-abiding being like me? Why, I lost a tentacle fighting in defense of peace——" As he talked, Blote moved toward the carrier.

"—your name, my dear fellow," he went on, "I'll mention it to the Commisssioner, a very close friend of mine." Abruptly the Vegan reached for a lever——

The long arms in the tight white jacket reached to haul him back effortlessly. "That was unwise, sir. Now I'll be forced to recommend subliminal reorientation during stasis." He clamped stout handcuffs on Blote's broad wrists.

"You Vegans," he said, dusting his hands briskly, "will you never learn?"

"Now, officer," Blote said, "you're acting hastily. Actually, I'm working in the interest of this little world, as my associate Dan will gladly confirm. I have information which will be of considerable interest to you. Snithian has stated that he is in the employ of Ivroy——"

"If the Ivroy's so powerful, why was it necessary to hire Snithian to steal pictures?" Dan interrupted.

"Perish the thought, Dan. Snithian's assignment was merely to duplicate works of art and transmit them to the Ivroy."

"Here," Snithian cut in. "Restrain that obscene mouth!"

Dzhackoon raised a hand. "Kindly remain silent, sir. Permit my prisoners their little chat."

"You may release them to my custody," Snithian snapped.

Dzhackoon shook his head. "Hardly, sir. A most improper suggestion—even from an agent of the Ivroy." He nodded at Dan. "You may continue."

"How do you duplicate works of art?" Dan demanded.

"With a matter duplicator. But, as I was saying, Snithian saw an opportunity to make extra profits by retaining the works for repeated duplications and sale to other customers—such as myself."

"You mean there are other—customers—around?"

"I have dozens of competitors, Dan, all busy exporting your artifacts. You are an industrious and talented race, you know."

"What do they buy?"

"A little of everything, Dan. It's had an influence on your designs already, I'm sorry to say. The work is losing its native purity."

Dan nodded. "I have had the feeling some of this modern furniture was designed for Martians."

"Ganymedans, mostly. The Martians are graphic arts fans, while your automobiles are designed for the Plutonian trade. They have a baroque sense of humor."

"What will the Ivroy do when he finds out Snithian's been double-crossing him?"

"He'll think of something, I daresay. I blame myself for his defection, in a way. You see, it was my carrier which made it possible for Snithian to carry out his thefts. Originally, he would simply enter a gallery, inconspicuously scan a picture, return home and process the recording through the duplicator. The carrier gave him the

90

idea of removing works en masse, duplicating them and returning them the next day. Alas, I agreed to join forces with him. He grew greedy. He retained the paintings here and proceeded to produce vast numbers of copies—which he doubtless sold to my competitors, the crook!"

Dzhackoon had whipped out a notebook and was jotting rapidly.

"Now, let's have those names and addresses," he said. "This will be the biggest roundup in TDMS history."

"And the pinch will be yours, dear sir," Blote said. "I foresee early promotion for you." He held out his shackled wrists. "Would you mind?"

"Well . . ." Dzhackoon unlocked the cuffs. "I think I'm on firm ground. Just don't mention it to Inspector Spoghodo."

"You can't do that!" Snithian snapped. "These persons are dangerous!"

"That is my decision. Now——"

Snithian brought out the pistol with a sudden movement. "I'll brook no interference from meddlers——"

There was a sound from the door. All heads turned. The girl Dan had seen in the house stood in the doorway, glancing calmly from Snithian to Blote to Dzhackoon. When her eyes met Dan's she smiled. Dan thought he had never seen such a beautiful face—and the figure matched.

"Get out, you fool!" Snithian snapped. "No, come inside, and shut the door."

"Leave the girl out of this, Snithian," Dan croaked.

"Now I'll have to destroy all of you," Snithian keened. "You first of all, ugly native!" He aimed the gun at Dan.

"Put the gun down, Mr. Snithian," the girl said in a warm, melodious voice. She seemed completely unworried by the grotesque aliens, Dan noted abstractedly.

Snithian swiveled on her. "You dare——!"

"Oh, yes, I dare, Snithian." Her voice had a firm ring now. Snithian stared at her. "Who . . . are you . . . ?"

"I am the Ivroy."

Snithian wilted. The gun fell to the floor. His fantastically tall figure drooped, his face suddenly gray.

"Return to your home, Snithian," the girl said sadly. "I will deal with you later."

"But . . . but . . ." His voice was a thin squeak.

"Did you think you could conceal your betrayal from the Ivroy?" she said softly.

Snithian turned and blundered from the room, ducking under the low door. The Ivroy turned to Dzhackoon.

"You and your Service are to be commended," she said. "I leave the apprehension of the culprits to you." She nodded at Blote. "I will rely on you to assist in the task—and to limit your operations thereafter to noninterdicted areas."

"But of course, your worship. You have my word as a Vegan. Do visit me on Vorplisch some day. I'd love the wives and kiddy to meet you." He blinked rapidly. "So long, Dan. It's been crazy cool."

Dzhackoon and Blote stepped through the Portal. It shimmered and winked out. The Ivroy faced Dan. He swallowed hard, watching the play of light in the shoulder-length hair, golden, fine as spun glass . . .

"Your name is Dan?"

"Dan Slane," he said. He took a deep breath. "Are you really the Ivroy?"

"I am of the Ivroy, who are many and one."

"But you look like—just a beautiful girl."

The Ivroy smiled. Her teeth were as even as matched pearls, Dan thought, and as white as——

"I *am* a girl, Dan. We are cousins, you and I—separated by the long mystery of time."

"Blote—and Dzhackoon and Snithian, too—seemed to think the Ivroy ran the Universe. But——"

The Ivroy put her hand on Dan's. It was as soft as a flower petal.

"Don't trouble yourself over this just now, Dan. Would you like to become my agent? I need a trustworthy friend to help me in my work here."

"Doing what?" Dan heard himself say.

"Watching over the race which will one day become the Ivroy."

"I don't understand all this—but I'm willing to try."

"There will be much to learn, Dan. The full use of the mind, control of aging and disease . . . Our work will require many centuries."

"Centuries? But——"

"I'll teach you, Dan."

"It sounds great," Dan said. "Too good to be true. But how do you know I'm the man for the job? Don't I have to take some kind of test?"

She looked up at him, smiling, her lips slightly parted. On impulse, Dan put a hand under her chin, drew her face close and kissed her on the mouth . . .

A full minute later, the Ivroy, nestled in Dan's arms, looked up at him again.

"You passed the test," she said.

THE WAR AGAINST THE YUKKS

1

Professor Peter Elton swung his machete half-heartedly at a hanging vine as thick as his wrist; the blade rebounded with a dull clunk. He lowered the black pigskin suitcase in his left hand to the spongy layer of rotted vegetation that covered the ground, took out a large handerchief with a faded machine-stitched monogram belonging to a fellow customer of the Collegiate Laundry and Cleaners, and mopped at his face.

"Constable Boyle," he called to the stocky, khaki-clad man whacking at the dense verdure ahead. "Are you sure you know where we're going?"

Boyle turned, flicked the sweat from the end of his nose.

"Absolutely, sir," he called cheerily. "Chased tht ruddy great jaguar right through this same ruddy thicket. Lost him at the river's edge—the Choluteca, that is. That would be about five miles ahead."

Elton groaned. He hobbled to a convenient log, sat, pulled off his brand-new hiding boots and began massaging his foot.

"But *we* don't have to go all that way, sir," Constable Boyle reassured him. "It was on the way back I stumbled over it; it can't be far from where we are at this moment."

"I can't help recalling my last ill-advised venture into the brush," Elton said. "An unspoiled Aztec site just twenty miles south of Texaco. We reached it after a fourteen-hour burro ride. After clearing away the greenery, I uncovered a Dr. Pepper sign, several hundred beer bottles, and the principle chassis members of a Model T Ford."

"This is the real thing, sir," Boyle said heartily. "Just

this column, like, sticking up; bloody great slab o' rock the size of a Bentley Tourer."

"And you're sure it shows signs of human handicraft?"

"Oh, that I can guarantee, sir." Boyle got out a well-worn hip flask, passed it across to Elton, who uncapped it and took a healing draught. "I hope you're not thinking of packing it home as a souvenir," Boyle went on. "You'd need a ruddy derrick."

"Nothing like that, constable," the professor said. "I've already told you I merely wish to examine it; make a few tests."

"I understand; that's what that bloody great case is in aid of . . ." He nodded at the heavy piece of expensive-looking luggage at Elton's feet. "I wish you'd let me carry it for you for a bit."

"No, no, I'll see to this, constable." Elton put a protective hand on the case. "The device I have here—which I developed myself—may well revolutionize the whole art of archaeological dating."

"That's a bit over my head, sir," the constable said.

Elton took another swig from the flask and handed it back. "With the chronalyzer—" he patted the case—"I'll be able to establish the ages of stone artifacts which have hitherto defied analysis. You see, the incidence of naturally occurring high-velocity particles on exposed rock surfaces induces submicroscopic changes in the internal crystal-line structure of the material; naturally, when a cut is made in a stone surface by man——"

"Who cares how old a blinking rock is?" Boyle cut in. "Now, *my* idea is, you can vet this thing, say whether it's worth the trouble of doing a bit of digging; then if we turn up anything—say a few solid-gold chamber pots——"

"Now, constable, I'm not interested in visionary schemes to defraud the authorities."

"Defraud, sir? That's rather a harsh term. As for meself, my salary as a blooming game warden is——"

"Is none of my business," Elton pulled his boots on and got to his feet. "I suggest we resume while the sunlight is good."

"As you say, sir. But it seems a shame, considering the

fact that we're a good fifty miles from Tegucigalpa and there's boats on the river to be had for a song."

"I don't sing very well," Elton said severely. "I have an adequate position with a reasonably good, small university and a full professorship in the offing if my chronalyzer proves out. That is the sole purpose of this expedition."

Boyle squinted at the sun. "We'd best be moving if we want to be back to Yuscaran tonight."

2

Late sunlight was filtering through high treetops where green parrots had set up a raucous evening serenade among the orchids when Boyle stumbled into a tiny clearing, yelled "Ha!" and pointed.

Elton came up beside him, his once natty bush jacket hanging damply, his solar topi on backward, his shins scratched. Before him, a two-yard thick cylinder thrust up from a tangle of flowering vines, its weathered surface almost obscured by a growth of grayish moss.

"Well, it appears to be artificial, just as you said," Elton commented. He gazed at the ten-foot high monument, circled it, studying the surface.

"Not much over a thousand years old, I'd guess," he said. "The Mayan stone-workers——"

"Why not try your apparatus on it and find out for sure?" Boyle suggested. "Then perhaps we might do just a bit of digging."

"No digging," Elton said firmly. He squatted by the case containing the chronalyzer, noting the scars and scratches in the once-splendid leather. He remembered the dinner the previous spring at which the luggage had been presented to him, along with a nice little check, on the occasion of his award-winning paper on *Some Evidences of an Advanced Technology Among Pre-Columbian Central Americans*. What would his colleagues say, he wondered, opening the case, if he returned from this trip with proof of the chronalyzer's success?

"Crikey," Boyle said, leaning over to peer into the case. "Looks like the insides of a reddy telly set."

"Oh, it's quite simple, really," Elton said, erecting the

folding tripod he had taken from the case. "I merely expose the surface in question to radiation of specific wavelength, and the resultant refraction patterns are interpreted by the sensor unit; the results are read directly from the screen here. Later, of course, it would be a simple matter to devise a direct-reading scale."

He lifted the chronalyzer from the case, settled it in position on the tripod, then flipped a switch and checked indicator dials. Power was flowing at the correct levels. He sighted through an eye piece, fine-focused the crystal-guided light source, then flipped down the toggle switch which bombarded the target with high-range ultraviolet. A beam of pale light made a gray spot on the curve of mossy rock. The constable stood at Elton's shoulder, staring at the wavering green glow of the four-inch square indicator screen, watching the wave-forms dance.

"What's that wiggly line mean?" he inquired.

"Hmmm." Elton studied the pattern, compared it with the scale taped to the panel above the glass. "Curious; the surface seems to date about eight thousand years back. That is, it was exposed to the open air at about that date."

There was a harsh, grating sound, a sense of vibration deep underfoot. Elton stepped back, looking startled. Before him, the stone seemed to tremble . . .

"Here, what's that?" the constable's voice had a note of surprise. "You feel that, sir?"

The vibration was very perceptible now. The stone was quivering visibly. Elton hastily switched off the chronalyzer with a loud *click!* A hairline crack became visible running from top to bottom of the looming cylinder. The crack widened; curved panels were opening out, sliding silently on oiled bearings. A bluish light winked on, revealing an interior chamber lined with fittings of an incomprehensible complexity.

"It's not . . . not one of these missiles, sir?"

A loud beep! came from the interior of the apparition. Elton jumped.

"Ascrabilik ahubarata" an inhuman, metallic voice said from inside the capsule.

"That's not Rooshian, is it, sir?"

"Definitely not Russian," Elton said, backing away.

"You had me fooled, sir," Boyle said. "Nice bit o' camouflage it was, too." He chuckled. "I'd of wagered you'd never been here before; a jolly good act you put on."

"Thank you, constable," Elton said in a squeaky voice, mentally picturing squads of armed security men pounding through the jungle to take him into custody. "*But how,*" he pictured himself asking, "*was I to know that there was a secret minuteman silo under this old rock . . . ?*"

"You scientist blokes," the cop said. "You're full of surprises." He shook his head admiringly.

"Yes," Elton mumbled, going into motion suddenly. "Well, thanks for your cooperation, constable. We may as well be running along now." He lifted the chronalyzer from its tripod, lowered it into the case.

"You're going to leave it like this, sir?" The constable's eyebrows went up.

"We're pressed for time," Elton said hurriedly. "We don't want to be caught out in the jungle after dark . . ."

"Ascrabilik ahubarata," the voice said again.

"Here sir, where's the voice coming from?" The constable poked his head inside the blue-glowing interior, his voice taking on an echoic quality. "What's——" A sharp buzz cut him off in mid-sentence. He stiffened, his arms jerking out from his sides; a dazed look spread over his face. A pair of bright metal clamps had extended from a receptacle, locked into the constable's head. Elton jumped forward, grabbed his arm and hauled at him. The buzz stopped abruptly, the clamps retracted. The constable staggered back, his hands to his head.

"Wh-what happened?" he choked. "Felt like my ruddy brains was being wrung out like a bar rag!"

"Mobile Command Center Ten Ninety-four, standing by for instructions," a harsh, high-pitched voice with a Middlesex accent said from inside the capsule.

"You might've warned me, sir," the constable said in a hurt tone.

"Uh . . . well, after all, these secret installations . . ."

Elton improvised. "But I'll explain it all as we hike out."

"MCC Ten Ninety-four, awaiting instructions," the voice said again. "On five minute standby alert, counting . . ."

"Where's the chap manning this show, anyway?" the constable asked. "They oughtn't to go off and leave it like this."

"Probably they just stepped out for coffee. No concern of ours, constable. Now, if you'll just give me a hand with the bag."

"Abandoned their post? Very strange, I'd call that, sir. Un-British. But then I suppose they're Wogs."

"MCC Ten Ninety-four awaiting instructions. Battle status, active."

"You hear that, sir? Blimey, do you suppose it's started? I knew that we couldn't trust those Russkis!"

"Just a routine exercise, I should think," Elton soothed, edging off into the surrounding undergrowth. "Now if you're ready——"

"Here," the constable said loudly, addressing his remarks to the capsule. "Constable Boyle here. What's this about a battle?"

"Battle report follows," the voice answered. "First Grand Fleet, annihilated, casualties total; Second Grand Fleet annihilated, casualties total; Third Grand Fleet . . ."

The voice went on, reeling off statistics.

"This is It, right enough!" Constable Boyle smacked a fist into his palm. "A hell of a fight going on somewhere . . ."

". . . Grand Fleet annihilated, casualties total," the voice droned on. "Sixth Grand Fleet, casualties ninety-eight percent; surviving units retired to defensive dome at station 92, under Yukk siege——"

"Ever heard of these Grand Fleets?" Boyle called to Elton. "That would be your lot, I reckon?"

"Certainly not," Elton said quickly. "Just code names; you know; the Blue Army versus the Red Army——"

"Never had any use for bloody Reds meself," Boyle stated flatly. "Well, if it's not you Yanks, it must be
99

British units involved. Always knew we were keeping a secret weapon tucked away someplace. Who'd have thought it'd be here in Honduras? But our chaps are in trouble, from the sound of it."

". . . Tenth Grand Fleet; Mobile Command Center Ten ninety-four standing by."

"Ten ninety-four? That's this apparatus here!" Boyle said excitedly. "And its ruddy crew's stepped out for tea!"

"If we hurry," Elton called cheerily.

"I don't like the sound of this," Boyle said. "Looks like the bloody Reds have had all the best of it, so far." He raised his voice to shout into the interior of the capsule.

"What kind of shape are the other blighters in?"

"Yukk Primary Echelon, annihilated, casualties total; Yukk Secondary Echelon, heavy casualties. Yukk Dreadnought *Abominable* operational, standing by off station 90——"

"Yukks, eh? Code name for the Russkis, shouldn't wonder," Boyle said. "And their dreadnought's got a group of our lads hemmed in at someplace called station 92. They'll be wanting a spot of help, sir!"

"Elements of Sixth Grand Fleet under siege at station 92. Besieging Yukk Dreadnought heavily outweighs units in ton/seconds firepower."

"W've got to get cracking, sir!" Boyle yelled. "We can't let the Bolsheviks wipe our chaps out!"

"Awaiting instructions," the voice said. "Three minute alert."

"Here, where's your station complement?" Boyle demanded.

"Station personnel departed to conduct local reconnaissance," the voice stated.

The constable whirled on Elton. "It's clear enough, sir; these chaps have buggered off and left their mates in the lurch. Lucky we happened along. It's awaiting our instructions!"

"Now, constable," Elton said reasonably. "Surely it's not talking to us——"

"Who bloody else? It popped open when we came along, didn't it?"

"I suppose my U-V triggered something," Elton muttered.

Boyle looked suddenly knowing. "Ah-hah, I think I see, sir. Security. You can't take action while I'm hanging about."

"Well, constable," Elton grabbed at the straw, "you don't expect me to violate NATO cosmic security?"

"I'll never breathe a word, sir, cross my heart!" Boyle was standing at attention, chin in, toes out. "We've got to give them a leg up, sir!"

"Out of the question, constable," Elton said, looking around for the first signs of flashing red lights, whooping sirens and pouncing military police.

"You're a cool one, sir," Boyle said stiffly. "Have to be, I suppose, in the counterespionage game. But it's not the British way to desert one's mates in time of need."

"One's mates? What in the world are you talking about? We've stumbled into some sort of war games, constable; if we're here when the authorities arrive, we'll end up in a maximum-security prison!"

"I'm saying it's the real thing, sir. Our boys are under fire. They're counting on us, sir!"

"What the devil do you expect me to do?" A strident note had entered Elton's voice, reminding him of his last interview with Dean Longspoon, in which the irascible department head had suggested that Elton spend more time in the classroom and less in what he termed exotic peregrinations. How right, Elton thought, the dean had been.

"We'll fill in for these blinking tea-drinkers!" Boyle proposed. "And I'll have a word for their superiors when this is over!"

"But—but——"

"Two-minute alert," the voice stated.

"I always thought when the chips were down you Yanks would stand with us," Boyle said. "I'm going in—alone, if I have to."

"But—it might be dangerous."

"Chance we have to take," Boyle said curtly. "Coming?"

Elton came slowly across to Boyle's side, looked into

101

the dim blue interior of the capsule, at a maze of pinpoint indicator lights, conduits, pushbuttons, fittings.

"Hmmm. Interesting layout. New type oscilloscope, subminiature fluorescents——"

"Awaiting instructions; one-minute alert before reverting to inactive status," the voice said.

"Go ahead, sir!" Boyle urged "I'm right behind you!"

Elton looked around; there were still no signs of aroused security forces bearing down. He put the suitcase on the ground, sighed and stepped hesitantly through the open entry.

3

At once, a folding seat deployed from the floor, nudged the back of Elton's knees, and he sat abruptly. Boyle crowded in behind him. Elton stared at the array of tiny dial faces and toggles, packed together like a display in a bargain jeweler's window.

"Say, you've got to hand it to those Air Ministry bods," Boyle said. "Not half crafty, that lot. Not a word in the papers about all this." He was looking around admiringly at the wilderness of quivering needles.

"Thirty-second alert," the voice stated.

"Wonder what that means?" Elton frowned.

"In twenty-five seconds, Mobile Center will revert to permanent inactive status if not activated," the voice said.

"You mean—we'll be out of the fight?" Boyle expostulated.

"Affirmative. Action must be taken within prescribed time limit, in accordance with standard anti-Yukk operational procedures."

"Suppose we don't?"

"Mobile Center will detonate. Fifteen-second warning."

Elton started out of his seat. "Fifteen seconds—let's get out of here!"

"We can't, sir!" Boyle caught his arm. "It's too late now to run! If it blows, it'll take us to kingdom come!"

"What'll I do?"

"Anything, sir! Just jab a button at random!"

Elton dithered, then lunged for the panel, depressed a fat red button directly before him. Instantly, metal bands snapped around his midsection, clamping him to the seat. Behind him, Boyle grunted, similarly restrained.

"Prepare for immediate jump to Battle Sector," the voice said emotionlessly. The curved door slid shut with a smooth sigh. The blue glow died, leaving only the jewel sparkle of the instruments.

"Hold on here," Elton yelled, tugging at the seat belt. There was an abrupt jar, an instant's pause—then a silent concussion that seemed to burst painlessly inside his skull. Boyle gave a choked shout—then all was silent and still again.

"S-sir?" Boyle got out.

"What . . . happened?" Elton managed.

"Sir, I've got a feeling . . . we're floating, sort of."

"Nonsense; the thing malfunctioned, obviously. Whatever was supposed to happen didn't. Perhaps it was never intended to. I'm beginning to suspect that we're the victims of the most idiotic practical joke of the decade!" Elton tugged at the seat clasp. "Now I suppose we're trapped here until they decide to come along and——"

"On station, Battle Sector Nine," the voice announced. "Request permission to deploy view screens."

"By all means, deploy the view screens," Elton said wearily. "And, by the way, just who the devil are you? Where are you speaking from? What's this farce all about, anyway? My name is Elton, and I demand——"

"This is the Lunar Battle Computer," the voice said. "I am positioned nine point three four two miles under the Lunar surface feature known as Mount Tycho. At your instruction, I have placed Mobile Command Center Ten ninety-four on station in Battle Sector Nine, four thousand miles off Callisto, on an intercept course with the Yukk Dreadnought *Abominable*. Request permission to deploy forward batteries."

"You mean—you really—I mean——" Elton tried twice to swallow, made it on the third attempt. "This *is* all some ghastly joke?" he croaked.

"Negative," the voice said flatly. It seemed to issue from a small slot set among the flashing lights—which were now blinking with renewed enthusiasm. A large amber X in midpanel winked on and off frantically.

"Callisto," Boyle said. "I've heard of it. Somewhere near Jamaica, I believe."

"Someone's idea of humor," Elton croaked. He managed a stifled laugh. "Why, if we were really four thousand miles off Callisto, we'd be hundreds of millions of miles away deep in space."

"Space, sir?"

"Callisto is—" he swallowed—"one of the moons of Saturn—or is it Jupiter?"

"Jupiter," the voice said tonelessly.

"Jupiter? Well, now, I knew our lads were holding something back," Boyle said complacently. "You Yanks and your moon shots are all very well, but here we British are, all the way out on Jupiter. Goes to show . . ."

"Goes to show what?" Elton yelped. "Suppose this thing knows what it's talking about? Do you know anything about piloting a satellite . . ." his voice trailed off in a squeak. Two translucent panels which had slid down from slots above, opened out, glowed briefly, then snapped into the crystal clarity of the finest photograph. Against a background of utter black, blazing points of light flared and sparkled. To the left, a brilliant curve of light like an enormous full moon edged into the picture. The screen above showed a similar scene, with the familiar tiny ringed disc of Saturn glowing, bright-edged, off to one side. In the center of the screen a moving blip glowed.

"There you are," Boyle said proudly, indicating Jupiter. "British soil, the whole lot."

There was a loug *ping!*

"What was that?"

"Yukk suppressor rays have locked on Command Center," the voice said in the same emotionless tone. "Likelihood of immediate salvo fire."

"Fire? You mean they're shooting at us? Goodness. Who would want to do that——?"

104

"Yukk dreadnought on closing course," the Lunar Computer announced. "Request instructions."

"Take evasive action!" Elton yelled. "Get us out of here!"

"Drive mechanism nonfunctional in field of Yukk suppressor rays," the voice said.

"Uh—fire the forward batteries!" Elton yelled.

"Guns nonoperative in field of Yukk suppressor rays."

On the screen the blip grew; it swelled visibly, bearing down at a headlong clip. Elton could make out details of the image now. A clumsy, double-pyramid shape, slab-sided, angular, rushing at him from dead ahead.

"Nothing for it but to ram, sir!" Boyle yelled. "God save the Queen!"

Elton lurched forward as the capsule seemed to brake suddenly. The pressure grew. Elton grunted as the seat clamp cut into his stomach.

"Yukk tractor rays now grappling Command Center," the voice said indifferently. "Request permission to self-destruct."

"Not bloody likely!" Boyle bawled. "We're not ruddy Kami Kazis!"

The pressure slacked off. The forward screen went dark, filled by the bulk of the Yukk dreadnought. In the rear screen the stars glittered and winked. A tremor ran through Elton's seat—a sharp jar, a sense of sliding, then silence again.

"We—we've stopped," Elton said uncertainly.

"What do you suppose it means, sir?" Boyle said in a strained voice. "I'd have wagered a fiver we were bound to collide with that monster."

"We're practically bumping into it now."

"We must be hove to alongside," Boyle said.

"I . . . I suppose they'll be along to collect us any minute now," Elton said.

"Captured," Boyle said disgustedly. "Without firing a shot."

"By the Yukks," Elton added. "We'll be brainwashed . . ."

"There'll be help on the way, sir," Boyle said cheerfully. "When the chaps we're filling for get back and find their machine missing, they'll be through to Air Ministry like a shot."

"I wonder what they're waiting for?"

Elton stared at the dark screen, unable to make out details of their captor. "I'd like to get on to the name-rank-and-serial-number part, and possibly get in touch with the Red Cross."

"Pity we're not armed," Boyle said. "We could have put up a spirited defense, and maybe taken a couple of the blighters with us."

Elton didn't answer; he was swallowing hard, running over speeches:

I am a civilian, captain; as a noncombatant, I insist—No, that would be hard to put over under the circumstances. How about: *Well, fellows, the fortunes of war, eh? Wonderful job you did at Stalingrad* . . .

"Maybe if you twiddle the knobs a bit, you can see something of what's going on out there," Boyle suggested. Elton tried the controls beside the dark forward screen; suddenly it lightened; a pitted surface of iodine-colored metal curved before them, sliding slowly past.

"That's better," Boyle muttered. "Don't imagine the Reds had anything like that! Bloody vast thing, isn't it?"

"Bigger than anything we've got," Elton said. "Alien-looking, isn't it? I wonder if Washington knows about this?"

"I should think Whitehall has likely let them in on it, sir."

"Listen," Elton said, "do you suppose that we somehow eluded their radar? After all, we're rather small, and they may have been expecting something their own size."

"You may have something there, sir." Boyle smacked his fist into his palm. "Hard lines we can't activate this blasted pogo stick we're sitting in."

"Look here, Lunar Computer," Elton said. "Isn't there a chance you can get us out of this spot we're in? It appears——"

"All systems now functional," the voice said.

"What! Why didn't you say so!"

"Data not requested," the voice snapped.

"Well, what about it. Can we jump away from here—get back where we started from?"

"Yukk suppressors are activated by high-velocity bodies moving within sensitivity range of instruments," the voice said flatly.

"Suppose we sneak away? Just sort of edge off-stage, so to speak?"

"What about the Commies, sir?" Boyle remonstrated. "If you're feeling a bit better now, we can renew the fight."

"Fight? Look here, Boyle, this has gone far enough. I must have been under the influence of alcohol. What kind of fight can this—this wandering phone booth put up against that Leviathan? No, thank you, I'll be happy just to get back, pay my fines, and leave quietly tomorrow aboard the *S.S. Togetherness* as planned——"

"Sir! Look there!" Boyle's fingers dug into Elton's arm; he pointed to the screen. In the section of the Yukk hull passing across the screen, a vast, gaping rent showed. Inside, Elton caught a glimpse of twisted structural members, buckled deck plates.

"No wonder they paid us no heed!" Boyle blurted. "Looks as though they had a spot of bother of their own." A second vast wound in the immense hull drifted into view. Great, blackened tubes that could only have been weapons hung in their carriages, silent.

"Crikey!" Boyle commented happily. "They've jolly well had it!"

"They're still active enough to deactivate our guns, shut down our engines, and take us in tow," Elton said. "The crew are probably all in the undamaged part, ready to blast us at the first sign of life."

"What about that, Looney Control?" Boyle barked.

"It's Lunar Control," Elton put in.

"Affirmative," the voice said.

"You see?" Elton said.

"Are they on the lookout for us?" Boyle pressed on.

"Negative."

"Why not?" Elton demanded.

"There are no survivors aboard the Yukk ship," the voice said casually.

"No survivors?" Boyle and Elton echoed together.

"Then," Elton said perplexedly, "who's been operating the suppressor, and tractor rays, and——"

"Yukk defensive armaments activated automatically at the approach of possible hostile bodies."

"Now you tell us!" Elton sagged in his seat. "Well, Boyle, I think that lets us off the hook. We can go back now."

"I wouldn't say so, sir," Boyle cut in. "What about those chaps under siege? We can't just go off and forget them."

"What siege? The Yukks have been wiped out. There's no one here to besiege them!"

"Perhaps they're not aware of their victory, sir! We've got to carry the good news to them. It'll be a feather in our cap, sir."

"I don't care for feathery caps," Elton said. "Let Lunar Control tell them, if it wants too—it seems to be damnably cagy when it comes to withholding information."

"All you've got to do is ask the right question, sir." Boyle's voice was smug. "After all, it's only a machine; admitted that itself. We're the only personnel here—and I say we have a duty to perform."

"All right, all right." Elton addressed Lunar Control. "Can you take us there—to wherever this Lost Batallion is supposed to be pinned down?"

"Station 92," the voice said "Affirmative."

"All right, I guess we'll give it a try. But creep along slowly, so as not to wake any sleeping electronic dogs. Where is this station 92, anyway?"

"On the surface of the moon Callisto."

"Miserable place to be marooned," Elton said, staring at the bleak expanse of wan-lit, cratered rock below. "Callisto is much too small to support an atmospere, and at this distance from the sun I imagine the rock never warms much above absolute zero."

The ground was moving up swiftly; the screens swept the close ragged horizon, fixed on the black of the sky. There was a lurch, followed by a thump.

"We're down," Boyle announced. "All right, open up," he called. "And——"

"No!" Elton yelled—too late. The seat clamps snapped back, the doors slid open—and a breath of cool, perfumed air wafted in from outside.

"It's—but—how . . . ?"

"Contact at station 92," the voice said. "You are now within the defensive force dome."

"Oh, that explains it," Elton let out the breath he had been holding. "The dome keeps the Yukks out, and holds the air and heat in."

"Now to spread the good word," Boyle said heartily. "Ready, sir?"

"I suppose you were right about coming over to let them know they've won." Elton stepped out, felt grass underfoot, sniffed the air. "My, won't they be delighted." He stared up at the heavens; Jupiter was a vast, pale crescent moon, glowing in banded pastel colors. Other, smaller moons moved visibly nearby. Vast numbers of fat, close stars glittered overhead.

"I wonder where they are?" Elton squinted into the deep gloom of the Callistan night.

"How many men have survived?" Boyle called to the capsule.

"Seven hundred and five individuals now occupy the redoubt," the slightly bored-sounding voice said. "None of them are Men."

"Did you say," Elton got out, "they're not . . . men?"

"Affirmative," the voice was bland.

"Blimey," Boyle said. "A bunch of ruddy Martians?"

"No wonder the Yukk ship looked alien," Elton groaned. "This is some kind of interplanetary war between intelligent oysters, or something. What are *we* doing mixed up in it?"

"Questions relating to organic motivations are not within my scope," the computer said.

"And the Yukks aren't Commies at all?" Boyle sounded disappointed.

"Negative, in the sense in which you employ the term; however, the Yukk practice a form of communal life, based on——"

"There you are, sir! Commies, as I said. These Reds are a crafty lot. As I see it, we British have made contact with the Martians, who've become our allies. It's a group of their lads out here, and it's our plain duty to carry on."

Elton scrambled back inside the capsule. "I don't know about you, constable!" he yelled, "but I'm leaving."

"Wrning," the voice said. "Yukk batteries command entire volume of space within ten million miles. Any attempt to jump will result in approach to Yukk vessel and consequent concentrated automatic Yukk fire with high negative probability of survival of Mobile Command Center."

Elton scrambled back out of the capsule. "Dandy," he said. "Marvelous. Rush to the assistance of our Martian allies, eh? *Now* look at the pickle you've gotten us in!"

"Me, sir? Why, I've merely lent a hand——"

"All right! But here we are—wherever we are—sitting ducks for the Yukk—whatever they are."

"Yukks; some kind of Bolsheviks, I don't doubt. But it's all the same to me. What we've got to do now, sir, we've got to make contact with our side and work out a plan of action."

"Never mind that," Elton said. "We've got troubles of our own. There's got to be *some* way to slip out from under the guns of that derelict."

"Not without first contacting these Martian chaps," Boyle protested. "We can take time to propose a toast or two, exchange cigarettes, that sort of thing . . ." Boyle's voice faded.

He stood, head cocked, listening.

"Do you hear anything, sir?" he whispered.

"Only you, making another fatuous suggestion," Elton replied tartly. "Personally, I favor asking questions of this mobile whatever-it-is until we get some useful answer, and then leaving as hastily as possible."

"There it is again, sir!" Boyle said.

"What?"

There was a sudden quick padding of feet, a loud whoosh!, a sharp chemical odor; Elton took a breath to shout, choked, felt the world swim out from underneath and fall on him like a vast feather mattress.

5

Professor Elton moved to get away from an unpleasant jogging sensation, discovered tight folds of coarse netting binding his arms to his sides and holding his legs in a tight crouched position. His left ear was pressing into the rough strands, and there was a sharp pain in his neck.

"Help!" he croaked. "Boyle, where are you?"

"Here, sir," a weak voice came back.

"What happened? I'm wrapped up like a mummy in some sort of seine."

"Same here, sir. We were took unawares, it appears."

"By your Martian friends, I suppose?"

"Look on the bright side, sir. We haven't been done in yet. That's something."

They were in a dim-lit corridor, Elton saw. By twisting his head, he made out the silhouettes of slender biped figures with immense heads. He was, he saw, trussed in a net slung like a hammock from the shoulders of a pair of the creatures.

There were shrill shouts from ahead, answering cries from his captors. More of the bipeds crowded around; Elton strained to get a clear view through the mesh, but carried as he was in a head-down position, he was unable to make out any more detail.

There was an abrupt lurching as he was carried up a short flight of stairs. He squinted his eyes against the sudden, brilliant light, then he oofed as the support dropped from under him, slamming him against a cool, hard floor. He pushed at the enveloping net, kicking it free of his feet, fighting it over his head.

"Good Heavens!" Boyle's voice burst out.

"Hang on, Boyle! I'm coming!" Elton shouted encouragingly. He flung the net from him, whirled——

"It said they weren't men," Boyle croaked.

Standing in a semi-circle facing the captives were six exceedingly pretty girls.

"Rubavilup mockerump hifswimp," one of the girls said. Elton reached up dazedly to adjust his tie, his gaze glued to the large greenish eyes in the pert face before him. Below the face was a slender neck, adorned with multiple strands of turquoise-like beads. A close-fitting, short-skirted tunic hugged nicely curved hips; a pair of shapely legs led Elton's eyes to the polished floor, where they paused for a moment, blinked and started back up.

"They're not bad-looking sir," Boyle said approvingly, "considering they're Martians."

The girl in the center of the group frowned. "Asibolimp hubshut ook?" she asked Elton.

"I'm terribly sorry, Miss," he said. "I'm afraid I don't understand."

"Here," Boyle said loudly. "Who's in charge here?"

"Aridomop urramin ralafoo glip?"

"Who's . . . IN . . . CHARGE HERE . . . ?" Boyle repeated, with gestures. The girls spoke briefly among themselves. One pointed to a door across the room, then took Boyle's arm, urged him on. He jerked free.

"Look here, my girl——" he started, shaking a finger under her nose. A sharp slap sent him back a step; his mouth opened and closed; then he reached for her. An instant later, having described a somersault over the girl's shoulder, Boyle gazed up from a supine position on the floor.

"Ralafoo glip," the girl said and jerked her head toward the door.

"I think when she says ralafoo glip she means it; better do as she says," Elton suggested, starting toward the indicated door.

"All very well for you Yanks, you're used to this sort of thing."

In the inner room, Elton followed gestures toward a massive chair placed against the wall, seated himself gingerly. Something cool touched the sides of his face just in front of his ears, pressed firmly. There was a sharp prickling sensation. Abruptly, his head seemed full with a screech like a tape recorder running backward at high speed. Elton flopped in the chair, caught by the head. As suddenly as it had begun, the screech ended; the clamps retracted. Elton stumbled to his feet.

"What in the name of the Fallen Towers of Hubilik was that?" he demanded, rubbing his ears.

"The language indoctrinator," the nearest girl said.

"I don't understand," Elton stated, staring from the girl to the chair. "How in the name of the Five Sacred Snakes of Bomakook did my sitting in that thing teach you to speak Grimblkpsk?"

"Umma oobabba ungha," Boyle yelled incomprehensibly, pointing at Elton. Two girls seized his arms, thrust him toward the chair. He braced his feet, still shouting nonsense. Elton saw the bright metal clamps swing down and grip the constable's head. They held him as he kicked out wildly, mouth open; then the chair released him. The girls stepped back.

"Now, if you'll behave yourself," the leading girl said to Boyle.

"Calm yourself, Boyle," Elton snapped. "I'm sure your behavior isn't helping us." He faced the auburn-haired girl who had first spoken.

"Now, young lady, if you'll just let me explain: My name is Rflxk . . ." he paused, frowning. "Rlfxk? Is that my name?"

"If you're honest, you have nothing to worry about, dearies," the auburn-haired girl said, taking his arm in a firm grip and steering him back out into the hall. "Our detectors showed us something has passed through the

113

screen. Naturally, we couldn't afford to take any chances. After all, you could have been Yukks—just like we learned in Training."

"Us Yukks," Elton managed a chuckle. "Why, my dear, we came here to assist you."

"Fat lot of good it did us," Boyle muttered behind him. "These bloody Amazons don't want helping."

"Assist us how?" Elton's auburn-haired captor inquired.

"Why, in the fight with the Yukks; but of course——"

"Ixnay, ir-say," Boyle said quickly. "One-day ell-tay em-they ut-way ee-way ound-fay"

"Well, back to the language indoctrinator," a red-head said.

"That won't be necessary," Elton said hastily. "My friend was just uh . . . reciting an old poem. By the way, where are we going?"

"A good luck spell? I hope it's a good one—not that they work."

"You're on your way to see the Mother."

"This is out of our jurisdiction," another added.

The girl holding Elton's arm looked up at him with a reassuring smile; her delicately curved lips were parted, showing even white teeth; her hair looked as soft as angora; her lashes were long and dark. With an effort he kept his eyes from the warm, rounded shape poking against his arm.

"We don't often get visitors from the other domes," she said. "It's kind of exciting, having you here."

"Why did you come?" another asked. "Is it about the fungus competition?"

"Now Nid, the Mother, will handle the interrogation."

6

The two men followed their escort along the high-vaulted corridor, up more steps and under a filigreed arch into a wide room, where dim light from lamps placed at random among deep chairs glowed on small tables with bowls of exotic fruits, cushioned chaise lounges, and, at the center of the room, a fountain that leaped up to fall back into a shallow pool in which a vast, pale-white figure reclined.

Two of the girls went forward, spoke briefly to the fat woman in the water. Elton could hear an answer in a hearty, policematron voice; the girls twittered again, pointing toward the two strangers.

"Let's have a look at 'em," the fat woman said.

Elton and Boyle moved up to the pool edge, averted their eyes in embarrassment as the matronly figure, totally nude, reached out for a fruit bowl at the poolside, selected a mango-like ovoid, took a large bite, chewed noisily.

"All right," the Mother said. "You did right, girls; they're an odd-looking pair; look a little weather-beaten; not what you'd call beauties; but they're not Yukks, that's easy to see. You there——" Elton knew she was talking to him. He faced her, arranging a faculty-type smile.

"We haven't seen strangers here in a long time," the woman said. "Especially the kind that barge in without warning. Why didn't your Mother call me? Never mind; good experience for the girls. Hearing about something in Training is one thing, actually seeing it's another. Now——" She took another bite of fruit—"you two girls just tell me in your own words what you're doing here."

"What do you mean, you two oof!" Boyle subsided as Elton's elbow caught him in the side.

"Well, ah . . ." Elton started.

"I don't believe I've seen your type before," the Mother said. "Flat-chested, aren't you? And narrow through the hips. You must have a hard time with your babies." She shot Elton a sharp look.

"Oh, ah, terrible," Elton nodded. "Actually, I've never——"

"What dome is it you're from?"

"As a matter of fact, we came here from Shrulp," Elton said. He blinked, trying the name again. "Shrulp?"

"Here, sir," Boyle put in. "Why not just tell them we're from . . . Shrulp." He looked puzzled.

"I've heard of Mumbulip Dome," the Mother was saying. "And we had a delegation from Rilifub Dome in my

115

Mother's time, after a rock tremor knocked out one of their air plants. They had a terrible time of it, crossing Outside in one of those old Travelers, afraid it would break down any minute; but Shrulp—that's a new one on me. Must be away over on Far Side." The Mother frowned. "You're not here to stir up trouble, I hope?"

"Goodness, no," Elton felt the smile slipping, twisted it back into position. "We understood that you needed help in the fight against the Yukks."

"Praise Mother," the woman made a cryptic sign with her hands, which the girls standing in her line of vision copied. She frowned at Elton. "Where did you get the idea we don't know how to deal with a Yukk?"

"Frankly—" Elton ignored Boyle's look, took the plunge—"the Lunar Battle Computer told us——" he broke off, seeing the expression on the Mother's face.

"Look here, young lady," the Mother snapped. "I'm as devout as the next person, but I won't stand for any superstitious nonsense. Now, I think you'd better explain your invasion of my Dome—and don't take me for a gullible old fool. I showed Mother Rilifub just how far she'd get trying to take the fungus arrangement championship away from us with her slick tricks."

"But it's nothing like that."

"Not that I don't respect the old ways, mind you. If it weren't for you troublemakers, the World woud be a peaceful place—and Girl has her place in it. But I'm not standing by to see charlatans get my girls all aroused. First thing you know, they'll be openly advocating Strange Ways——"

A gasp ran through the assembled girls. The old woman ignored the reaction, signaled to a pair of handmaidens standing by. They stepped forward, gripped the fat arms of the Mother and heaved her to her feet. She puffed, wading to shore.

"Tikki, Nid," she said to the attendant girls, "I'm tired. I'll talk to these girls later; they've put me all on edge, and I want to be calm if it comes to a Judgment. Take them along and mind you keep them under close surveillance." She accepted a vast huck towel, draped it across her shoulders, waddled to a chair.

116

"You'd better give them a blanket apiece and lock them in a storeroom," she added. "You know how crowded we are for space . . ." She shot a hard look past Elton at the girl Tikki. "Yes, I hardly know how we're going to find room for them, with crowding the way it is. But we'll manage somehow. Meanwhile, I intend to check with this Shrulp Dome wherever it is. If they're here to spread Strange propaganda . ." She gave Elton a look which reminded him of a portly Dean of Women he had once known, who had suspected him of intent to impregnate her charges.

"But we haven't told you——" Elton started.

"Silence!" the fat woman snapped. "I'll talk to you later. Maybe tomorrow."

"See here, we came here to do you a good turn, and without even listening, you're talking about locking us in storerooms."

"If they haven't taught you proper respect for Mother at Shrulp Dome, you'll learn it here!" The Mother said sharply. "Take them away, girls!"

Back out in the corridor, Elton cleared his throat and tried again.

"Pardon me, but aren't you girls concerned about the Yukk dreadnought out there, aiming its guns at you right now?"

"You girls must be overly preoccupied with theology eover at Shrulp Dome," the girl the Mother had called Tikki said. "Sure, we know all about the Yukks, but after all . ." she winked at Elton. "Nobody's ever really seen one. So why should we worry?"

"I don't understand," Elton said. "Here you are, right in the midst of a terrible battle with some sort of ghastly monsters with huge ships the size of mountains—and you don't seem to care."

"If we're good girls, they can't hurt us," the girl dismissed the subject. "Listen, you seem like nice enough girls. The Mother said to lock you in a storeroom, but . . . maybe we could work something out." She turned to speak ina low tone to the girl beside her. They turned into a side corridor lined on both sides with identical doors; it

117

had a deserted air. Through a half-open door, Elton caught a glimpse of an empty room, daintily furnished in bright, flashing colors.

"Look," Tikki said, "I'll tuck you in my room. Even though we're awfully crowded, as the Mother said," she added. "It won't hurt if we double up, if you don't mind sharing the bed. You must be simply worn out from the trip. I'll bet it's just awful outside the Dome," she shuddered.

"Sharing . . . your bed?" Elton asked.

"It will just be for tonight. Your friend will go with Nid. Tomorrow one of the other girls will have you, and the night after that another."

Elton took a deep breath. "Well, if you're sure it won't put you out?"

"It'll be fun," the girl said. "We can just cuddle up and have a nice long talk. I want to hear all about Shrulp."

7

It was a small, neat room, with fluffy curtains at the window, a shaggy rug on the floor, a flounced spread on the bed, and a rack in one corner on which hung a dozen bright-colored short tunics. Elton's hostess took off her turquoise beads and hung them on the rack, eyeing Elton's battered bush jacket.

"My, those are certainly strange-looking clothes you have on. I suppose you needed them for the trip, but you can get out of them now. I'll draw us a tub. Would you like a little ginger in it or maybe a touch of mint? I always like mint, myself."

"Tub?" Through an open door Elton saw a pink-tiled room, and tropical-looking flowers in planters lining a ten-foot square sunken pool with bright chrome fittings.

"We can just relax and scrub each other's backs," Tikki said. She finished undoing the snaps down the back of her tunic, shucked it off, dropped it in a wall slot, faced Elton wearing a diaphanous one-piece undergarment.

Elton's collar suddenly felt tight. He felt his face break into a silly smile. "Well, whatever you say . . ."

118

Tikki plucked a small box from a table, offered Elto what looked like a plastic cigarette. He groped, took one, jabbed it at his mouth. Tikki took one, drew on it, blew out perfumed smoke. "I'm afraid you bugged the Mother, with all that talk about the Yukks. She's a dear, really, but very hard-headed when it comes to religion. She says it's time we did away with outmoded concepts and recognized that the Yukks are merely an externalized personification of an inner yearning for defilement, or something."

"Look," Elton said abruptly. "Let's play a little game. We'll pretend I just arrived from . . . from someplace so far away that I never even heard of the Yukks, or the Mother, or the domes—and you tell me all about it," Elton said.

"That sounds like a very strange game," Tikki said doubtfully. She opened the door to an adjoining room, stepped inside; a moment later a sound of rushing water started up. Steam wafted into the room, carrying a scent of Life-savers. Tikki came back, holding a large cake of violet soap.

"Is that what you play back at Shrulp?"

"Yes, we spend a lot of time telling each other things we already know. The trick is to catch the other . . . ah . . . girl in a mistake."

"Well, it doesn't really sound like much fun. If you feel like playing, wouldn't you rather just wrestle? I'll bet you know some interesting holds."

"Maybe later," Elton gulped. "Now, you were going to tell me all about the Yukks, remember?"

Tikki put a finger to her cheek, nibbled at her lower lip, looking thoughtfully at the ceiling. Elton found the expression perfectly delightful.

So was the slim, tanned body below it.

"Well, nine hundred and sixty-four—or is it sixty-five . . . ? Let me see." Tikki nibbled a fingertip. "It must be sixty-five because I finished Baby Training when I was ten, and Girl Training when I was eighteen, and it was sixty-one then, and that was four——"

"Sixty-five it is," Elton put in. "You're doing fine."

"Anyway, nine hundred and sixty-five cycles ago, when the war with the Yukks was in its nineteenth cycle, there was a great battle fought between two fleets. Now, in those days there were many among the girls who were badly tainted with Strange Ways."

Her voice, Elton noticed, had taken on the tone of a pupil reciting lessons. "Because of this, the girls weren't able to destroy the wicked Yukks, as they deserved. Instead, the Great Mother sent a terrible thing called a Disruptor that caused the machines of the girls to malfunction, and all of the girls were killed or captured—except one shipload. The captain was a righteous Mother, and so she and her girls were spared. They landed here on the World, and set up the Force Domes, and the defensive screens, to keep the Yukks at bay. That's why it's our duty to tend the Field Generators, and defend girlhood, and weed out any traces of . . ." she blushed, ". . . Strange Ways. Not that anybody has any," she added.

"Any what?" Elton asked.

"Strange Ways," Tikki said primly. "You know."

"But we're playing that I don't know, remember?"

"Here," Tikki said reaching for Elton's top jacket button. "I'll help you get these things off. The tub's ready by now." The stream had formed a pinkish haze at eye level. "Is this what holds it?" She undid the button clumsily. "I'm not very good at this . . ." She undid another button.

"What about the Yukks?" Elton's voice sounded strained. Tikki undid the last coat button and pulled the garment off him.

"Well, the Yukks are evil beings who tried to enslave all Girlhood, once, long ago, before we were driven out of the Heavenly Garden. They were great big ugly creatures, with hair growing all over their faces, and huge, bony hands—six of them, I think—and whenever they could catch a poor, defenseless girl, they'd . . ." Tikki swallowed, her face pink. "They'd do Strange Things to her."

"Strange Things?" Elton's voice was a squeak. Tikki was just finishing the last shirt button. She peeled it back over his shoulders.

"And the terrible power they had was, that they made perfectly nice girls *want* them to do the Strange Things. Even now, there's always the danger that a girl will fall into Strange Ways—like dreaming about a Yukk chasing her, with all six hands reaching for her—and even catching her . . ." Tikki took a deep breath. "That's what makes the Yukks so terrible, and that's why if there really ARE any Yukks, and one of them ever managed to get into the Dome—" Her eyes were flashing with anger; her nostrils flared—"everyone would tear the horrible hairy thing into tiny little pieces before he could spread any Strange Ways!"

"Tiny little pieces?" Elton stammered. He grabbed for his shirt, pulled it back on. Tikki's eyes strayed to his chest. "My you *are* flat-chested," she said, in an envious tone. She put a hand under each of her magnificently formed mammaries, looked sadly down at them. "These DO get in the way . . ."

Elton was backing toward the door. "Ah . . . I've just remembered something," he blurted, fumbling the door open. "Where did they take my friend? I have to find hi—her—right away!"

"Oh, she's just next door," Tikki said. "But——"

Elton whirled to the adjoining door, banged on it, twisted the knob. It flew open. Boyle, shirtless, was just reaching for the tanned curve of his hostess's hip.

"No!" Elton shouted.

Boyle yipped and jumped a foot into the air.

"I've got to talk to you!" Elton hissed, "privately,"

"Look here, can't it wait?" Boyle's face had assumed a beefy color. "Bloody cheek, I call it, bursting in here just when I was about to . . . to . . . make friends."

"That's what I have to talk to you about." Elton glanced at Boyle's roommate, then at Tikki, standing in the doorway, looking puzzled. "Do you mind, girls? Just for a moment?" He ushered the girls out, closed the door. "I've made a discovery," he started.

"Me too," Boyle said, smirking. "I think we're on to a good thing. A different one every night, at that. Now if you'd just toddle off, there's a good lad——"

"Do you know what they do to Yukks if they catch one?" Elton cut in.

"Tear 'em to bits, Nid said—that's my young lady. They've no more use for bloody Reds than—"

"Correct," Elton said. "They tear them to pieces. Small, hairy pieces."

"So what's that to do with us?"

"Plenty," Elton said. "We're Yukks."

8

Boyle was sitting on the bed, mopping at his face with a tiny lacy hanky he had found under the pillow.

"That was a near thing," he said. "Another five minutes——"

"And you'd have stood revealed as the ancient arch-enemy of girlhood," Elton said decisively.

"But look here, from what Nid said, they've been living here on this Tup'ny world for nine-hundred cycles, whatever those are."

"Nine hundred and sixty-five," Elton corrected him. "I think the term probably refers to Jupiter's revolutions around the sun. That would be about . . . hmm . . . eight thousand two hundred years, Shrulp time."

"Eight blinking thousand years? But that Looney Control affair said the crew had just stepped out."

"They did, too—about the time the ice was melting off Wisconsin. Probably ran into a party of early head-hunters or a wandering hyaenodon. I'm afraid Lunar Control has little or no awareness of the meaning of time."

Boyle shook his head. "Eight thousand years with no Yukks? Then how in the Six Rivers of Blue Mud do they have blinking babies?"

"I'd imagine they have a supply of frozen sperm—or possibly they've developed a method of parthenogenesis."

"How do you suppose this bloody system ever got started?" Boyle looked bewildered. "What this lot needs is a firm masculine hand to put things in order. I've a mind to——"

"To be torn to bits? Please, Boyle, this situation requires careful handling. We've got to get away from here—that much is clear. And there's no time to lose. Sooner or later someone is going to put two and two together."

"And it may as well be me," Boyle said with sudden decision. "Leave that Nid to me for a night or two and I fancy——"

"Strange Ways," Elton said. "That's what they call that sort of thing. I suppose it all started with some sort of idiotic feminist movement, somewhere. The women developed a method of reproducing without men, and declared their independence. Naturally, war followed; a war fought in space."

"Why space? And how? There weren't any bleeding space vessels eight thousand years ago."

"Apparently there were. As a matter of fact, I did a paper once—but never mind that. Being women, the girls wouldn't want to do anything as untidy as fighting a war right there on Earth—and then too, I suppose the important logistical targets were off-planet; control of the spaceways was the key to success. And so a great battle was fought, and both sides virtually wiped each other out. The surviving girls reached Callisto here, and set up these force domes and a defensive screen to keep off what was left of the Yukks; and the Yukks, with only one damaged ship left mounted a siege; then they died off—but the girls never knew."

"I see . . . and back home, everybody made up and forgot the whole thing."

"Not quite; there's still a certain residual hostility. But the economic drain of the war and the loss of personnel plunged society back to a minimal cultural level—and we're only now reattaining their level of technology."

"All right, granted you're on the right track; what do we do now? Slip out of here and leg it back to the Mobile Whatsit?"

"We don't even know where it is—and anyway, the Yukks have us pinned down, remember? The minute we come out from under the defensive screen, blooie!"

Boyle chewed the inside of his cheek; a shrewd expression settled over his features. "They won't shoot—not if we let them know we're Yukks ourselves."

"Maybe," Elton said, looking thoughtful. "We *could* give it a try, I suppose."

"No time like the present." Boyle went to the door, opened it. Nid and Tikki came in, two slim creatures as unself-conscious as a pair of young antelope.

"What are you two girls talking about in here?" Tikki asked.

"I'll bet you have some important message from your Mother?" Nid hazarded.

"As a matter of fact, we do," Elton said. "Of course, this is a very confidential matter. You mustn't tell anybody."

"Not even Mother?"

"We tell Mother everything," Nid said.

"Even about your—Strange Thoughts?" Elton hazarded.

Nid and Tikki blushed a delicate shade of purple.

"We'll have to confide in you ladies," Boyle said solemnly. "We've got wind of a big push the Reds are planning. High Command is counting on us. We have to go back to our traveler."

"You mean—there really *are* Yukks?" Nid's eyes were large with wonder.

"Absolutely," Elton nodded.

"I . . . I feel all sort of wiggly inside." Tikki put her hands to her stomach.

"Can't you wait till in the morning?" Nid asked anxiously. "It's only a month away."

"No, we have to go right now."

"Even before our bath?"

"Definitely."

"You're such brave girls," Nid said admiringly.

"I . . . I can't go," Tikki said. "I'm afraid I might—" Her lip quivered. "I might turn out to be—unreliable." She burst into tears.

"There, there." Elton patted her shoulder, dismayed. "What's there to be afraid of? You'll be with us."

"You don't know what an awful girl I am," Tikki sniffled. "I have Strange Thoughts all the time . . . and I'm afraid . . . might . . . I might . . disgrace Mother." Her sobs took over. Nid took her hand. "Now, Tikki, you're not the only one. I don't know a girl who doesn't have a Strange Thought now and then."

"B-but I have them all the time . . ."

"I'll tell you a secret: So do I; but——"

"But I *like* them!"

"Look, we'll keep an eye on you," Boyle said. "You'll have to shut down that salt-water factory now, we'e got to get cracking."

Tikki dabbed at her eyes and looked at Boyle resentfully.

"Why, you're the meanest girl I ever met," she said.

Elton stepped up and put a protective arm around her.

"Just leave Tikki alone, Boyle. Can't you see she's upset?"

"Too right," Boyle muttered. "Let's be off, Nid, me lass. No time to waste, you know. Mother's orders and all that."

Nid opened the door and peeked out. "Coast is clear," she said. "What about you, Tikki? Coming?"

Tikki looked up at Elton. "I'll go," she said, still sniffling. "If you'll promise to . . . to watch me."

"I won't take my eyes off you."

"Good. I'll feel safe then." She squeezed Elton's hand. They stepped out and started off along the hall.

Twenty minutes later, the foursome rounded a fountain tinkling in the dark, stumbled past a six-foot hedge, saw the blue glow of the Mobile Command Center ahead.

Elton halted. "There aren't any guards on it, I hope?" he whispered.

"Of course not? Why should there be?" Tikki said aloud.

"Shhh!" Elton cautioned. "This is a top secret mission, remember."

They came up to the capsule sitting quietly, doors open, waiting.

"Looks like everything's shipshape," Boyle said. "Just like we left her."

Elton leaned close to him. "Stand by with the girls a few yards back. I'll try to arrange a truce."

"Right," Boyle moved to comply. Elton stepped into the cramped chamber, settled into the seat.

"Ah . . . look here, Lunar Computer. I'd like to contact the Yukk ship, get a message to their computer; whatever it is that controls the vessel. Is that possible?"

"Messages can be transmitted on the Yukk wavelength."

"All right; I want to tell them I'm taking off, and not to shoot. I want them to know we're on their side. Tell them we're Yukks, just like they are, and——"

"MADAY, MADAY," the metallic voice screeched. "Yukks occupying Mobile Combat Command Center Ten Ninety-four! Executing emergency procedure forty-one!" Elton's seat lifted, dumping him out onto the grass. With a hiss and a sharp *smack!* the doors closed, snipping off the blue glow. There was an abrupt *zing!* followed by a small thundercap. A gust of wind ruffled Elton's hair. The capsule was gone.

"Here!" Boyle yelled. "What do you think you're doing?"

Nid and Tikki stood staring.

"It . . . it went off and left us," Elton said weakly.

"Did I hear it say . . . Yukks?" Nid demanded.

"W-where are they?" Tikki asked, looking around.

"Now we've had it," Boyle groaned. "Stranded, among these Yukk-eating females!"

"What did you say?" Nid demanded.

"Never mind, my dear. You've been as nice a little friend as a girl could have. Now just run along and let me think."

"Hold on, Boyle," Elton said, getting to his feet. "Don't panic." He turned to Tikki. "You girls don't happen to have another Traveler like ours—do you?" he asked hopefully.

The girl shook her head. "I never saw one like that before."

"Do you have any kind of . . . of space vessel?" Elton said desperately. "Anything you can use to travel up there?" He jabbed a finger at the night sky.

"We have one . . ." Nid said doubtfully. "But——"

"That's all we need," Boyle said promptly. "Just lead the way, there's a good girl."

"Well . . . it's a funny time to be going to church."

Distantly, Elton heard the shrill of a siren. Far away, someone shouted.

"Oh, dear," Tikki said. "Someone's discovered you girls have gone out without permission, I'll bet. Mother's going to be upset."

"Let's just hurry along to the ship—quietly," Elton urged. "After all, we can't let anything interfere with the mission, can we?"

"I think we'd better tell Mother," Nid said doubtfully.

"No time," Boyle said. "Every minute counts. Mother will understand, won't she, professor?"

"That's what I'm afraid of. Let's get going!"

"This way," Nid said, and slipped away into the shadows, the others at her heels.

A vast, clumsy pyramidal shape loomed up, the base stretching away into darkness. Elton came up to it breathing hard, listening to the clang of bells, the shouts of *Yukks* and the shrill ululation of the siren.

"They're pretty well stirred up," Boyle said. "How do you reckon we get inside this beast?"

"Where's the door, girls?" Elton inquired, peering through the gloom.

"Over here," Nid called. At Elton's side, Tikki shivered. "It's scary," she said. "I have the feeling the Yukks are right here beside us."

Ahead, Boyle muttered a curse. "Watch that bottom step, professor; rotted through." Elton gave Tikki a hand up, followed her up a short flight of crumbling wooden steps; as he stepped through the wide entry, his shoes clanged on metal.

"Where's the bridge, or the cockpit, or whatever you call it?" Boyle asked in a hoarse whisper.

"You mean the Mother's seat?" Nid asked. "This way . . ."

Elton and Boyle grunted and puffed, clambering up narrow campanionways in the dark, banging their heads on low passages, snorting dust from their nostrils.

"Bit of rum odor about the place," Boyle commented.

"It reminds me of the smell of the Royal Chamber in Cheops' pyramid," Elton said.

"Here we are," Tikki said. "What are you going to do now?"

There was a shout from below, an answering call, then a mutter of conversation.

"How do we close the entry port—the doorway?" Elton hissed.

"That's this big handle over here," Nid said. "Are you going to hold a Service now?"

Elton grabbed the dimly seen lever, hauled it down. There was a growl of metal. Below, a heavy *clang!* cut off the voices.

"Wish there was a bit of light here," Boyle said.

A wavering, yellowish illumination sprang up. Tikki smiled from the panel, where scattered indicator lights glowed wanly. Elton went over, stared at the layout.

"Tikki, do you understand all this?"

"Oh, certainly; we had all this in Training."

"How do you start the engines?"

"Oh, goody, we're going to have a Service." Tikki turned to the panel, reeling off details of the countdown checklist. Boyle came over, holding a thick book in his hand.

"Have a look at this, sir; the log, I imagine."

"Later," Elton said. "You'd better give me a hand here, Boyle. This is pretty complicated."

Boyle listened in silence for a moment.

"Hold up there, Tikki," he said. "Look here, professor, this is hopeless. It would take a ruddy genius to gen up on this drill in the time we've got. You see what we have to do, don't you?"

Elton looked at him. Tikki had stopped her recital and was listening, eyes wide.

"You mean?" Elton said.

"Right! They've got to go along. Couldn't let them back outside anyway, without letting that lot down below in."

"But—that would be kidnapping."

"Tikki!" Nid's voice came suddenly, a shrill yelp. "Look!"

Tikki jumped up. Nid rushed to her, thrust a faded and curled sheet of flexible plastic into her hand. Elton craned to see it.

KNOW YOUR ENEMY! the heading read. Under the legend was a clear, glossy full-length photograph of a nude Yukk.

Tikki looked from Elton to Boyle, back to the picture. "It . . . it looks . . . like the new girls," she said in a quavering voice.

"Just look at that flat chest," Nid gasped. "And those skinny hips; and—and . . ."

There was a heavy thumping from below. Boyle whirled to Nid. "Look here, love, there's no time to give you the full story now; just get this machine going, there's a good girl!"

"We . . . we really ought to go for help," Nid quavered.

"Start the ship up, Tikki," Elton pleaded. "Even if we are Yukks, we're not such monsters, are we now?"

"But I don't . . . I mean, why——?"

"With that crew snapping at our heels, I should think it would be bloody obvious!" Boyle snapped. "You said you know how to operate this thing! Hop to it, or we've bought the ruddy farm!"

"I'm a wicked, wicked girl," Tikki said weakly. "I'll do it . . ."

She went to the control panel, seated herself in the padded chair, punched buttons, closed switches; lights winked and glowed sluggishly; instrument needles stirred from pegs; there was a dry *click!* somewhere. Tikki got to her feet.

"There," she said. "But I just don't see how you can think of ritual at a time like this——"

"What ritual? We just want to depart as quickly as possible," Elton reached for Tikki's hand. "I hate to kidnap you like this, my dear, but——"

Tikki shivered and leaned against Elton. "I keep having the Strangest Thoughts . . ."

There was a final thump from below, a screech of reluctant hinges, then a babble of voices. Feet thumped on stair rungs.

"They're inside!" Elton urged Tikki toward the panel. "Quick!"

A girl appeared at the control room door; Boyle jumped at her, came staggering back as she stiff-armed him. More girls crowded into the room; a heavy-set fortyish woman pushed through, stood with hands on hips eyeing Elton and Boyle.

"So you're Yukks," she said in a loud, deep voice. "You don't look so tough to me!"

Elton lunged for the panel, punched buttons at random. Two of the girls pulled him away.

"A religious nut," the deep-voiced woman barked. "Well, it's too late for that, you! And anyway, you Yukks have no business desecrating the Church!"

"Church? She said it was a ship," Elton stammered. "The only one there was . . ."

Boyle groaned. "It just came to me," he said. "No wonder nothing happened when Tikki twoddled the controls. This must be the ruddy vessel this lot came here in, eight thousand years ago."

"So the story goes," the captain said. "Now let's get moving, you two." She shot Tikki and Nid a hard look. "And there'll be an investigation into the role you girls played in this escapade, too."

"We . . . we kidnaped them," Elton said.

"A likely story." The woman jerked a thumb toward the frightened girls. "Put all four of them under guard and march 'em back to the dorm. It looks like the Mother's going to be sitting in Judgment tonight."

9

The Mother was reclining in a heavily padded chaise lounge, with a box of pink and yellow candies at one elbow and a plate of cookies at the other. Heavy robes with elaborate flounces obscured her ample contours. She looked at Elton severely.

"Lying to the Mother," she said. "You ought to be ashamed, even if you are Yukks—and I never thought the Enemy would turn out to be so insignificant-looking."

"They're worse than they look," the captain of the guard said. "You see the state they've got this pair of ninnies in," she indicated Tikki and Nid, standing by with drooping expressions.

The Mother's face tightened. "I thought from the first there was something Strange about them." The assembled girls—several hundred of them, Elton estimated, all ages, crowded into the wide Mother's Room—sighed in unison.

"Silence in the courtroom!" the Mother snapped. "This is an open-and-shut case. These two are Yukks—that's plain enough. They led a pair of formerly decent girls astray," she eyed Tikki and Nid. "I'm going to let you two off lightly; cold baths every three hours for the next two days; that ought to cool those Strange Ideas off." She turned back to Elton and Boyle.

"As for you, there's only one way to deal with a Yukk: it's out in the Cold for you——"

The crowd of Girls gasped; a murmur ran through them. Tikki sprang forward.

"That's perfectly horrid!" she cried. "If they're going out in the Cold, I'm going too!" Strong-arm girls jumped for her, dragged her back in line. Nid was sobbing quietly. Doyle shot her a sickly smile. "There, there, lass, don't fret."

Elton cleared his throat. "Just a minute, Mother," he said loudly. "Berore you take this drastic step, I think there are a few things you should know."

"What's that? What could a Yukk have to say that would interest a Mother?"

Elton folded his arms, a calm, self-confident expression on his face.

"If you'll clear these others from the room," he said easily, "I'd like to tell you the Facts of Life."

Elton was lounging at ease in a deep-cushioned chair that was a twin to the one the Mother had occupied at the Judgment, eating large hot-house grapes that were being popped into his mouth one at a time by Tikki, while other girls crowded close.

Wide double doors opened across the room. Boyle appeared, shaved, his hair curled, a neat short tunic flapping at his thighs. A bevy of shapely girls surged around him, all chattering at once. Two ran forward, scattered varicolored cushions in a heap by the side of the wide pool set in the floor.

"I've got to give you credit, professor," he said. "You look like a blooming oriental potentate. How in the name of the Nine Gates of Ishalik did you do it?"

Elton wrinkled his nose. "I think they overdid it a bit with the perfume, Boyle," he said easily. "Otherwise you look well."

"The old bitch was ready to shove us outside the dome without even a set of earmuffs," Boyle stated. "We'd have frozen solid before we had a chance to asphyxiate. What did you say to her to rate us all this?"

"Girls, leave us!" Elton said, waving a hand. "You can come back in a few minutes, dears."

They fled, casting longing glances back.

"Well?" Boyle demanded.

"Elementary, my dear Boyle. Surely you noticed the large number of rooms in the dormitory wings? Several hundred in our wing alone, and I saw at least a dozen wings——"

"Don't talk ruddy architecture. Get to the point!"

"This *is* the point. There are only seven hundred and four girls here—and yet the building was obviously designed for many more. And then there was the business of the Mother chattering about the crowded conditions; consigning us to a broom closet."

"That was just a bit of bloody cheek," Boyle said.

"No, it was important to her to give us the impression that the dome was overflowing with girls; these domes don't get along too well with each other, remember. She

132

didn't want strangers to find out her fighting strength had fallen so low."

"Well, if it's low, it's her own ruddy fault. I reckon she's the one that controls the birthrate."

"Hmmm, yes—as far as she can. But did you notice Boyle, that there are no children around? Tikki and Nid are about twenty-one; there's quite a number about the same age. The next grouping is at about the forty-five age level; the older generation, I suppose. Then there are a few old ladies who——

"But there's no new generation, Boyle, and none of the girls are pregnant."

"So?"

"They've been using an artificial insemination method—using frozen sperm cells, all of the x-x variety—thus only girls were born. But unfortunately, the supplies ran out twenty-odd years ago."

"Blimey! Then——"

"Exactly. After eight thousand years, it was all over—until we came along."

"So now it's up to us?"

"Correct, Mr. Boyle. I suggest we work out some sort of equitable division. It should take us a year or so to work our way through, and then start over."

"Of course," Boyle said doubtfully, "it means we're stranded."

"Not forever. I learned from the Mother that there are very extensive libraries here, well-equipped laboratories——"

"Hold it!" Boyle leaned on one ebow, looking worried. "These little ones we'll be fathering: half of them will be little Yukks!"

"Of course. Things will come back to normal in about twenty years—and by that time I think we'll be ready to retire. We'll set up schools, start training a new generation of technicians. They'll be able to get the old ship going again—or build a new one. We can neutralize the Yuk ship, return to Earth in style with enough technology to make us too rich to talk to." Elton picked up a dusty book from the floor.

"But, this is my greatest prize," he said. "The log book from the ship. It gives an excellent picture of the pre-history of human affairs on Earth from about 15,000 B.C. up until the war seven thousand years later."

"Twenty years, eh?" Boyle mused. "But look here, pro-fessor, I just happened to think! All the old bag had to do was take a specimen from one of us—there's millions of germ cells."

"But she didn't know that, Boyle—so we'll just let it be our little secret."

"I think you've hit on it, professor," Boyle called. "Never tell 'em all you know."

"Correct," Elton said. "And in the meantime, we'll deal with our problems . . . one at a time."

GOOBEREALITY

Barnaby Quale, imaculately clad in pale yellow Gooberalls and ochre Gooberbund for his meeting with the head of Goober Enterprises, sat on the edge of the vast, hard chair reserved for personal interviewees of Harlowe Goober, waiting for the magnate to speak.

"Environmental Simulator?" Goober's voice combined the toughness of Gooberplast with the silky texture of Gooberlon. He fixed Quale with a daggerlike glance from pale blue eyes magnified by quarter-inch electrolenses, prodded the sheets of sketches and calculations before him.

"I'm a practical man, Clune," he announced. "Never went in for this what-d'ye-call-it science stuff; a Goober hires men for that. Now suppose you leave out all the technical talk and state just what it is you're referring to."

"It's the matter I wrote to you about, six months ago, Mr. Goober," Barnaby said. "It's a new application of cybernetic theory. By harnessing a data-response syndrome to a manipulative device, using an application of the principle that's employed in the Goobervendors to synthesize a variety of products——"

"I'm familiar with the function of the Goobervendor, Gorm," the industrialist barked. "One of my finer contributions to the Great Society, ranking just after the Goobertape and just ahead of the Gooberlator." He lit up a Gooberfitter with a flourish.

"Yes, sir," Quale nodded. "But my device does more than merely produce a product to specification. It assimilates the data introduced, collates, interrelates, extrapolates and, on the basis of up to one hundred billion separate informational factors, re-creates the exocosmic matrix implied by the observed phenomena———"

"Boil that down to straight American, Clud!" Goober snapped. "I have an appointment in two minutes with the Secretary of Poverty. The program's being expanded to cover another hundred million newly qualified citizens, and Goober Enterprises will be expected to make its usual massive input to the common good." He clamped the cigar between large, square teeth and glared at Quale.

"I was wondering, Mr. Goober, if you've had time to look over my calculations and designs, and reach a decision about backing me."

"Ah, I think I recall something of the matter now, Grudd. You're the fellow who quit us to go off on his own! Some wild scheme to mock up some sort of mechanical wax museum."

"Mr. Goober, I don't think you've quite grasped the real significance of the Environmental Simulator! It's not just a gimmick! It's a research tool of the first importance! There are dozens of applications for the device! Police forces could use it to reconstruct crimes, on the basis of all available clues; historians can fill in gaps in historical situations by setting up all known data. The Simulator will fill in the gaps by extension of the known———"

"Nonsense, Greeb! A visionary scheme! Totally impractical! Goober Enterprises wouldn't put a nickle into a crank idea like this!" Goober rose, a vast, massive figure in fashionable purple Goobervelt with a touch of Gooberlace at the wrists.

"One of my people will show you the way out."

"I know the way out," Barnaby said. "I worked here for six years."

"And having deserted the firm, you now come crawling back for handouts!"

"I'm offering you a solid business deal," Quale protested. But Goober was gone, in a swirl of Gooberfumes.

Barnaby made his way from the Executive Wing, rode the Gooberlift down to ground level, took a shortcut across the Experimental Complex toward the Research Block. A new shed had been set up, he noted; a huge, slab-sided structure covering an acre or two of ground. A

136

tall, thin man emerged from a tiny door set in one corner.

"Say, Barney," the man hailed, "what you doing over here? Haven't seen you in months."

"Hello, Horace. Just been in to see the Old Man about my proposition. He turned me down cold."

"Say, that's too bad, Barney. Looks like he'd pay a little more attention to the man that gave him Goobervision, Goobertape, Goobertronics, the Goobervendor."

"All I did was supply the ideas, Horace; Mr. Goober got them into production. By the way, what's this?" Barnaby waved a hand at the looming structure.

Horace looked grave. "This is something big, Barney. It's called the Goobernetic Goobereality Simulator. Very hush-hush."

"Simulator?" Barnaby's eyebrows rose almost to his hairline.

"Sure. A great concept." Horace looked around. "Come on inside," he said in a conspiratorial tone. "I'll give you a peek."

Barnaby followed Horace through the door into the echoing vastness of the immense structure. Fifty feet overhead a roof of translucent Goooberplast admitted a warm, golden light. To the left was a bank of massive machines, featureless in gray housings, a control booth beside them. Otherwise, the flat, covered acres were as smooth and featureless as a parking lot.

"This one was the Old Man's own, personal idea," Horace said. "It came down right from his office, about six months ago. Top priority. We rushed her through. She's all programed now, ready to go. He plans to give a demonstration for the industry tomorrow; I've got an idea he's working an angle to get a Cabinet appointment out of this one."

"What does it do?"

"Damnedest thing you ever saw," Horace said. He led the way to the control booth, indicated a wide panel. "You feed in your data here; it's flashed to the main cybernetic banks over in Vault One, and processed. See that big cable there? A direct tap to the main power pile. You got over 50 Goobermegs to draw on. When the red light goes on, you throw in the main switch here; that activates the Simulator, and starts the mockup going——"

"Horace—you mean—it sets up a simulated environment?"

Horace gaped. "Hey, how'd you know that?"

"Look, Horace, are you *sure*? I was just talking to Mr. Goober——"

"Oh," Horace looked relieved. "He told you about it. For a minute I was afraid there'd been a leak."

"You said there'll be a demonstration tomorrow?"

"Sure, we're all ready to go. We've already run complete tests; works like a charm. You'd swear it was the real thing."

"I suppose there'll be representatives from the leading universities here—and maybe the FBI and the Secret Service——"

"Huh? Heck, no, Barney. This is a hush-hush deal. Goober Industries stands to clean up on this one. The only ones invited are Hashflash Associates, Tosscookie & Wilt, and Earp, Earp, Earp & Earp——"

"Why, those are all advertising agencies!" Barnaby frowned. "What interest would they have in an Environmental Simulator?"

"Are you kidding? Talk about market research! With this setup, the advertiser can penetrate right into the innermost secrets of the American scene! No more wondering what brand underarm the typical family uses; just plug in the data, and take a look!"

"But—but, Horace! He couldn't! That's invasion of privacy! And it's a perversion of the intent of the device! I meant to make a lasting contribution to human knowledge."

"You, Barney? What've you got to do with it?"

"What? Look, Horace, this is *my* invention—the one Mr. Goober just turned down!"

"Huh? Hey, wait a minute, Barney! Are you kind of hinting around that Mr. Goober would—well—*swipe* your idea?"

"It looks that way—and it also looks like he's planning to use it to sell more Gooberjunk. I intended the Simulator to be used for human betterment—not for prying into people's personal business."

138

"Personal business? What personal business? After all, with everybody on the Government payroll——"

"*We're* not on the Government payroll; you work for Goober Enterprises and I'm in business for myself."

"Uh-huh, same difference; Goober Enterprises does all its work on Government contract and you're registered under the Poverty Act. After all, since the hundred percent income tax went through, a fellow doesn't really have much chance on his own, does he?" Horace chuckled. "No, Barney, if you want to have a Great Society, you've got to give up a few luxuries like privacy."

"But people have some rights."

Horace wagged a finger. "Now, Barney, you can't work for Uncle Sam, live in Government housing, subsist on Government handouts, and still babble about rights, now can you?"

"Look, Horace—could you give me a demonstration?"

"Not a chance, Barney! I shouldn't even have let you on the lot. Like I said, this is under wraps."

"But I've got to see how it works! After all, it's my invention."

"You want to get me fired? Let's go, Barney. I got to lock up."

An hour later, in his cubicle on Shelf One-oh-two, Slice Six Hundred and Fifty-five, Stratum Nine, Block Seventeen of Number Forty-two Bachelors' Barracks, Barnaby looked around in annoyance at a buzz from the Gooberscope. He flipped a lever; a pert girl's face appeared on the foot-square screen.

"Oh, hi, Gigi, what do you want?"

"Barnaby! Is that polite? How did the conference go? Is old Gooberpuss going to finance your invention?"

"Hah! He already has! It's ready for a big demonstration in a day or so."

"Barnaby! That's wonderful! Why didn't you tell me?!"

"The only trouble is he's squeezed me out of the picture. He's passed out the word that it's all his own idea; and when I tried to go back and demand an explanation, they told me he was in Patagonia on a big Gooberblubber negotiation."

"Why, the old crook!"

"Look out, Gigi, these Gooberscopes may be Goober-bugged. You'll lose your job, and then there'll be two of us on relief."

"Barnaby, he can't do this! You can go to court, make him pay you——"

"Sure—if I had the price of a couple of high-powered legal firms. Goober has a hundred and forty-five of the top shysters in the country on the payroll, with nothing to do but sit around inserting fine print in contracts and fighting damage suits. Anyway, I'm not really sure it's my Simulator; I didn't see it working."

"What are you going to do, Barnaby?" Gigi's voice rose to a wail. "You've worked on this for three years! This was going to be your big prize! We were going to g-get m-m-married . . ."

"For heaven's sake, don't cry, Gigi!"

"All these years you've slaved, and old Gooberface has gotten rich off your ideas!"

"No, he hasn't; his whole salary goes for taxes, just like everybody else's."

"I don't mean his silly old salary! What about his expense account, and his representational allowance, and his Government bonuses and——"

"Sure, he lives like a king—but I'm not interested in that. All I want is to prove a man can still make it on his own. Every time I think about Goober stealing my ideas and then giving me the brushoff, I see red!"

"Now, Barnaby, don't do anything hasty!"

"Hasty? After three years' work? I'm going over there and make him pay up if I have to sit on him an pound his head on the Gooberug in his own office!"

"Barnaby! Wait!"

"I'm going. So long, Gigi!"

"Then I'm going with you. I'll be down in five minutes!"

The vast Executive Tower was dark when Barnaby and Gigi left the subway at the Gooberdilly Circus stop and emerged into the wan light of early evening.

"See? I told you we'd be too late," Gigi said. "The executives never work during prime TV time."

"There are lights over at the Experimental Complex; maybe Goober's there, gloating over how he robbed me!" He led the way across to the gate, spoke to the guard on duty.

"Sure, Barney, no harm in letting you look around. Hi, Gigi." He waved them past. Inside, they headed toward the shed that housed the Goobernetic Goobereality Simulator.

"Barnaby, you can't go in there," she cautioned. "You know these sheds are top secret."

"Naturally! Goober doesn't want to advertise stolen goods!"

"Please, Barnaby, come back tomorrow, and discuss the matter in a gentlemanly way with Mr. Goober. Maybe he didn't mean——"

"How can I, when he's in Patagonia?" Barnaby reached for the door.

"We're trespassing!" Gigi wailed. "Let's go now, before somebody sees us . . ."

Barnaby twisted the knob; the door swung in; he stepped into the darkened interior of the shed.

Gigi's voice echoed in the wide gloom. "Barnaby! We have no business in here!"

"There's nobody here, Gigi; relax."

"Where's your invention? All I see is a big open space . . ."

"Over there; that's the computer console and the synthesizing units. You see the wires strung around the shed? They tie the whole space into a closed field. I must say, he did a first-class job of installation. All I had in mind was a little thing about the size of a phone booth."

"Do you know how to work it?"

"Naturally; it's a dead steal from my drawings." He stepped inside the control booth. "All you do is set up the coordinates you want; the Simulator does the rest."

"Barnaby! You wouldn't! Mr. Goober would be furious!"

"Not any more furious than I am."

"But—but it's all set up for tomorrow's demonstration!"

"Sure, that makes it simpler. I'd better check out the

instrument readings first . . ." Barnaby studied the panel. "Looks okay; all we need to do is punch that button." He pointed.

"Barnaby, wait!"

He stepped past her and closed the switch.

For a moment nothing happened; then a dim light sprang up all across the enclosed space under the luminous Gooberplast ceiling; a deep humming sound was audible, rumbling from some subterranean chamber.

"Boy, look at those power drain figures!" Barnaby breathed.

"What's happening, Barnaby?" Gigi said breathlessly.

"The field is energizing. It's soaking up power like a sponge; that's to be expected, of course. Energy/matter conversion isn't an easy proposition."

There was a deafening boom! followed by a whistling of air. The door to the control booth rattled in its frame. Suddenly an opaque, gray blanket seemed to hang over the observation window.

"Barnaby! Is everything all right?"

He peered out into the mist. "I think so. Readings are all normal."

"Why is it so—so foggy out there?"

"The field shuts off incident light; it's a sort of closed space effect. The simulated environment has to be segregated from outside influences, of course, or its validity will be compromised."

"Barnaby, you've done enough for now. Let's go. We can come back some other time——"

"Go? We haven't even looked at it yet."

"That's all right; we can go up to my place and I'll make you a nice cup of coffee substitute and——"

"We can't leave now, without even seeing what kind of effect we've gotten." Barnaby stepped to the door marked AUTHORIZED GOOBERMEN ONLY and opened it. He stared out. Gigi came to his side. Where the plain concrete floor had been, a city street was visible, lined with bright shop fronts thronged with people.

"Wow!" Barnaby breathed.

"Where—where did the people come from?" Gigi

whispered. "And those shops——"

"I knew it would be good," Barnaby said in a choked voice. "But this is fantastic . . ."

"Let's go back," Gigi said.

"Let's take a look," Barnaby said. He took her hand and stepped out into the street.

It was midday, and bright sunlight gleamed down from above. The passers-by jostled them in normal fashion, hurrying about their simulated business.

"It's marvelous!" Barnaby said. "Goober's technicians fed in data for a contemporary 1972 street scene, it looks like. The Simulator extrapolated, built up he charge on the environmental field, and boom! Here it is, perfect in every detail!" They strolled along, admiring the view. The pedestrians ignored them, forcing them to dodge to avoid being rammed.

"Are they—real?" Gigi asked.

"Of course not. But they'll behave as if they were." Barnaby snorted. "And Goober plans to use all this to figure out what kind of depilatory has the greatest appeal. And I suppose he'll lease it out to politicians to overhear what the typical voter is saying about the issues, and——"

"Are they just false fronts? Is there anything behind the facades?"

"Certainly; they'll be perfect, inside and out."

Gigi gave a shrill cry. "Barnaby, look! The control room! It's gone!" Barnaby stared back the way they had come. The street seemed to dwindle away into the distance.

"What happened to the control room?" The girl gasped

"Oh, it's right there where it always was, but the closed-space effect keeps you from seeing it. Actually, we're in a sort of little universe of our own here, held together by the terrific power flowing over the surface of the field——"

"I'd feel a lot better if we could see, Barnaby. What if we got lost here?"

Barnaby laughed. "Nonsense, Gigi. All we have to do is go in a straight line to any of the walls, and . . ." he frowned. "No, that's not quite right; the field curves space

. . . but if we just go back to the control room . . . but . . ."

"Barnaby! What's the matter! You look so pale!"

Barnaby swallowed hard. "Nothing—nothing at all. But maybe we'd better just find that door right away . . ." He turned, walked quickly back, groped at the empty air. A stout lady in runover shoes puffed past, ignoring him. He worked his way across the sidewalk, turned and looked back.

"I'm *sure* it wasn't this far along," he muttered.

"Barnaby, we were standing at least over there when we stepped into this place," Gigi said worriedly, pointing. "I remember the crack in the sidewalk."

"You must be mistaken, Gigi." Barnaby indicated a stout oak door set in the wall behind him. It bore a brass plate reading CHAST & SEEMLY STUDIOS, LIMITED.

"Let's try in here," he called. He opened the door, held it for Gigi. Hesitantly, she stepped inside. They were in a narro foyer, discreetly lit, austerely decorated, unobtrusively air-conditioned. Sterilized music murmured from an indefinable source.

"Look," Gigi said. "Elevators. Where could they go? There isn't anything above . . ."

"Appearances are deceiving; we're still inside the field. If we go up, we can look out of a window, and then maybe we can see the outer walls. That will tell us where we are."

"Well . . . maybe."

Barnaby pressed the button; there was a soft whoosh! of air. The doors slid aside. They entered the car.

"Four floors ought to be high enough," Barnaby said. The car moved up, eased to a stop. The doors opened. Barnaby looked out into a dimly lit residential-looking corridor, deeply carpeted, neuter-toned, silent.

"Hmmm, I guess we'll have to look around and find a window." Barnaby stepped to a blank oak panel, rapped on it. Nothing happened. He tried it. It swung open. They stepped through and stopped dead, staring. Sun streamed through lacy curtains over wide windows where flowers grew in pots. On a brand-new stepladder by a sootless fireplace set with a gleaming brass shovel and poker, a well-muscled man of twenty-five with the features of a god, wearing well-pressed dark slacks and a perfectly fit-

144

ted polo shirt spread a hideous pink paint on a white wall, using an immaculate brush. The paint flowed out in a flawless swath with each stroke. A beautiful girl in a starched white blouse and red slacks wielded a roller in the lower section of the wall. Her work was, if anything, more perfect than his. Not a drop had been spattered.

"This Kem-tone is the paintier paint," she stated. "Goes on so easy, your friends will think you called in a high-priced decorator——"

"Pardon me, folks," Barnaby said. The two home decorators ignored him. He went to the window, looked out. sheet of cardboard with a lithograph of a seed-catalog garden blocked the view.

The man on the stepladder turned to dip his brush. Barnaby stepped up to him. "Hey!" The man went on painting the same spot, in smooth effortless strokes.

"Comes in twelve delicious colors, too," the girl commented. "Lemon, lime——"

"Look!" Barnaby said. "This is an emergency. We're lost. Can you tell us——"

"Maybe they can't see us—or hear us either," Gigi suggested in an awed whisper.

"They'll hear me," Barnaby said determinedly. He seized the man's painting arm; the ladder tilted; the man swayed, crashed to the floor, upsetting the girl in red slacks who fell sideways, still painting unhurriedly. Lying on his side, the man worked his brush imperturbedly, laying a pink stripe across the girl's chest. She rolled her roller in the air, smiled with pink features as the brush worked over her face.

". . . . Strawberry," she cooed. "Raspberry, prune, chop suey and chicken noodle . . ."

"Let's get out of here!" Barnaby seized Gigi's hand, charged across the room, burst through a door. They were in a sunny breakfast nook. A lovely girl in a ruffled apron stood with her head sideways, one hand on hip, holding a coffee pot.

"More Chase and Sanborn's?" She smiled brilliantly.

A man with incredibly regular features looked at her happily from his chair at the table. Before him on a machine-decorated plate a symmetrical fried egg lay beside

145

two geometrical strips of bacon. He held a clean starched napkin in his left hand. He rolled his eyes ludicrously, his tongue curling over his upper lip; he wrinkled his nose . . .

"Ummm, ummm," he said feelingly. "It's my favorite . . ."

Barnaby looked about for another door. The wall ended just beyond the table. Holding Gigi's hand, he plunged for it, jarring the table. Behind him, the man smiled as steaming coffee poured down on his knee.

The two rounded a partition, almost fell over a finely gowned woman who tilted a can of chemical over a toilet bowl. "Since I discovered new Drano," she said brightly, "Old-fashioned, inferior products have been banished . . ."

A man stood watching, a finger digging at the back of his neck, a cap between his fingers. He appeared slightly ill with malaria, and his overalls needed pressing. A number of large, new, tools lay scattered on the floor at his feet, together with brushes with bent bristles, bottles and cans with blurred labels, and a large and unsightly rubber plunger. He wore a marvelously intricate expression, compounding ruefulness at having been outdone by a housewife, admiration of new Drano, shame at his use of old-fashioned, inferior methods, and determnation to learn from the experience, all overlaid with a smile.

Barnaby cleared his throat. "Say, can you give us a hand?"

"Next time, Lady, it's new Drano for me," the man said.

Barnaby twitched the can from the woman's hand, upended it in the plumber's hip pocket.

". . . embarrassing bathroom odors, too," the woman said gaily. Smoke poured from the plumber's pocket.

Barnaby and Gigi ducked between wet sheets on a clothes line, one gray and one white, and made for a plain door. It opened, and they stepped into a vast room with a high shadow-trussed ceiling. At its far end, television cameras were grouped around a floodlit set. The two stepped silently behind a heavy tan curtain that hung among ropes and wires, crossed the room, peeped out at the set, not more than twenty feet away. A man sat behind a broad polished desk, a green-painted wall behind him. To the left of the desk was a large gold-fringed American flag, and on the right was a blue flag with an eagle in the center and lettering around it. Barnaby read between the folds:

.. SID ... OF THE ... TED ... TES .. MERI ...

The man reached out to shuffle papers, glanced toward a wall clock. Barnaby stared at the gray hair, the ski-jump nose, the wide bluish jaw.

"That man," he whispered. "He looks just like Nixon."

Nixon was talking: ". . . opportunity to make this report on my recent trip, and the meetings which I held with President de Gaulle, and Chancellor Brandt, during which we discussed . . ."

"Goober's cooking up some kind of political plot here!" Barnaby hissed, turning to the girl. "People will see this, and think it's the real Nixon——"

Gigi clutched at his arm, looking frightened. "Barnaby, let's go . . . !"

"They can't get away with this," Barnaby said. He stepped from behind the curtain, went toward the desk. Nixon ignored him.

". . . easing of world tensions. We were in agreement—wholehearted agreement—as to the goals to be sought. The means——"

Barnaby looked around, picked up a broom and swung it. "Scat!" he said. The desk microphone spun to the floor; papers flew. Nixon went on unperturbed:

". . . necessitates renewed dedication on the part of each and every . . ."

Barnaby swung again. Nixon bounced from the chair, glossy silver hair still in place. ". . . taxation. However, in the near future, I have every hope . . ."

The imitation Nixon lay on the floor, legs drawn up in sitting posture. ". . . forces of Godless Communism . . ." Barnaby flailed at it, saw dust fly from the neat dark-blue suit. ". . . threat of war . . ."

We brrught the heavy end down on the head of the puppet. A round glass eye rolled across the floor. The blue jaws moved: ". . . the free peoples . . . The free peoples . . . The free peoples . . ."

"Barnaby, stop!" Gigi cried.

147

"Goober must be planning on taking over the country," Barnaby called. "He's got this dummy set up to look like Nixon, and he's broadcasting it over TV. No telling what kind of conspiracy we've stumbled into here." He looked around, spotted a fire hose coiled against the wall. "Maybe a blast from that will slow things down. Dupe the American people, will he?" He lifted the hose from its bracket, stretched it across the floor, hurried back and turned the valve. A surge of water whipped the heavy canvas hose like a scorched python. Barnaby leaped for the nozzle, wrestled it into position as a spurt of water spewed forth, then fought to hold it down as a hard three-inch stream arced across the caverrnous dim-lit room. The door opened, two men stepped through it, snapped over on their backs as the water hit, carrying along those behind them. Barnaby concentrated the stream on a skinny woman with a shrill voice, now raised in a patriotic number. He hosed her out the door, then cut the footing from under a fat man.

The water gushed, swirling around the light stands and cameras; sheets of white paper were afloat now; people scrambled to their feet to be knocked spinning by Barnaby's stream. Now another jet joined the first as Gigi unlimbered a second hose, giggling.

"Let's leave 'em squirting and get out of here," Barnaby called gaily. He propped the hose, holding it in place with a heavy TV camera stand, quickly set Gigi's hose up to add its volume to the attack.

"There's a door there," he pointed. "Let's try it." He sloshed through the water to the small door marked EXIT in red light, found it locked. The water was ankle deep now. They tried another door.

"These hoses really put out," Barnaby said. Nixon floated past, bumped against a floodlight stand. ". . . the free peoples . . . the free peoples . . ."

The next door Barnaby tried swung open. Beyond it were stairs. They started down; dirty water flowed down the steps with them. At the ground floor, they went through a swinging door into a room filled with tall clattering machines. Rows of empty bottles advanced along moving conveyors, paused under chrome-plated nozzles that gushed red, yellow, purple, then moved on under an arm that hammered a cap on each bottle, whok! whok!

People appeared across the room. Barnaby took Gigi's hand, jumped on the nearest conveyor. Bottles flew and smashed; green liquid jetted, spattering. They leaped to the next belt. It broke; they scrambled on to the next. Behind them, bottles poured off onto the floor in an endless stream; purple liquid spurted, foaming.

"They're closing in on us!" Barnaby called over the clank of the apparatus, the crashing of glass, and the hiss of foaming beverage. "Throw bottles, Gigi!" He scooped up an armful, hurled them at the machinery; they hit and bounced off, shaatered on the floor. One bottle lodged in a conveyor belt, crushed as the belt entered a slot. A moment later, there was a loud clunk! The belt piled up, writhed off onto the floor. More bottles tumbled.

Atop the machine, Barnaby saw a large valve near his hand. He turned it. The flow of orange pop increased. He turned it farther; the pop flooded out, boiling up in sudsy billows. He jumped to the next machine, twisted the valve. Purple suds mingled with orange. Gigi saw, added red foam. The attendants moved placidly about their work, now lost in bubbles, now emerging, froth-covered but undisturbed. Barnaby leaped down to the floor near the outer door, plucked an uncapped bottle from the line.

"Thirsty work!!" he said. He took a gulp, frowned, tossed the bottle into a group of whirling gears that ground to a halt with a screech of metal. "Let's get out of here . . ."

In the street, they looked back. Dense smoke poured from the top-floor windows.

"Looks like we started a fire, knocking over those arc lamps," Barnaby said. "Maybe it will attract attention and somebody will cut the power off."

"The fire is getting bigger!" Gigi called. "Look! it's leaping out the windows!"

A bell clanged, and a large red fire engine lumbered around a corner, pulled to a stop. Men in oilskins broke out hoses, connected up to hydrants. A stream of white

149

water started up, played over the building, found a window; steam billowed. Another stream joined the first.

"This is fun!" Gigi cried. "I've never seen anything like this before!"

A torrent of water surged from the front entry of the burning building, carrying paper plates, Sunday funnies, television schedules. A man washed out the door, a golf club in his hands. Bobbing in the flood, he shook his hips, kept his head down and swung, sending a shower of water over Barnaby and Gigi.

"Those imitation people are well made," Gigi said. "They're waterproof and everything."

A Good Humor man pedaled from a side street, his bell tinkling faintly amid the hubbub. Barnaby stepped forward, tipped him from his seat, caught the coasting vehicle. The man paddled solemnly, lying on the pavement.

"Chocolate or strawberry?" he called cheerfully.

A second pumper appeared, sending a sheet of water up as it whirled to a stop. More water poured into the windows. The smoke was denser now, the flames were visible leaping up above the roof.

"They're losing ground," Barnaby said. "The fire is gaining." Water was flowing out over the first-floor windows now. Paper clogged the gutters. In the street, the water level rose, topped the curbs. A desk floated from the building, then a chair, then a cluster of foam-rubber bras.

"We'd better get moving," Barnaby said. "The fire is into the next building; the water's rising fast!"

"Can't we watch a little longer?" Gigi asked. Nixon floated past.

"The free peoples," he said. His hair was still nicely combed. "The free peoples . . ."

"Not unless you want to swim for it!"

Gigi followed as Barnaby led the way up an alley that debouched into a wide street.

"Into the park," Barnaby called. "We'll be clear of the fire there—and maybe we can see where we are!"

They scaled the fence, crossed a wide lawn, made their way along the edge of a stream. Passing a screen of trees, Barnaby held up a hand.

"I hear voices."

They stepped back behind the trees. The voices came more clearly, now:

"Darling!"

"Sweetheart!"

A man and girl appeared, walking arm in arm. He wore a sturdy windbreaker, corduroy pants with tight legs, gum-soled shoes. His hair was cut short. He was very handsome. The girl's wind-blown dark hair was tied with a violet scarf; she wore a suede jacket and a bright woolen skirt. She looked up at him with adoring eyes.

"Down by the water," he said. "Sweetheart."

"Oh, darling . . ."

They came down the slight slope, found a secluded place on the grassy bank, sank down.

"Now . . ." the man said. He unbuttoned his jacket. The girl's lips parted, her eyes bright with expectation and longing. He leaned closer to her.

"We'd better get out of here," Barnaby muttered.

The man stretched out his hand to the girl. There was a candy bar in it.

"Have a Welch's" he said.

"They had me fooled," Barnaby said, stepping out. He went over to the couple, plucked the candy bar from the girl's fingers. They paid no attention.

"I hope this isn't one of those awful marshmallow centers," he said, offering a bite to Gigi. He patted the imitation man's pockets, ". . . rich, creamy goodness," the fellow was saying.

"Damn. No cigarettes," Barnaby said.

"Yes, and with Welch's, quality comes first," the female said softly, baring her teeth and taking a bite of empty air.

Barnaby and Gigi resumed their stealthy progress, emerged from between trees onto a graveled drive that swept in a graceful curve before a white-columned mansion. Half a dozen rich-looking people clustered around a small, cheap, but very shiny car.

"Say, that's an idea," Barnaby said. "We can cover ground quicker in that."

151

They crossed the lawn to the group.

. . . luxurious cardboard interior," a gorgeous red-head purred.

"And so economical, too," a trim-moustached ambassadorial type said.

"It's what's under the hood that sells ME," an effeminate-looking undergraduate offered, raising the hood to look wonderingly at the tiny engine.

Barnaby toppled him, slammed the hood down. He helped Gigi in, then slid into the driver's seat, started up, gunned down the drive, swept through an open gate and out into a wide avenue.

The street was crowded. Barnaby slowed. A stream of traffic crowded toward a red light suspended over the street ahead. He looked curiously at the cars. They were immense, wide, low, plastered with great strips and shapes of bright chrome work, rusty at the edges.

"I never saw cars like those before," Barnaby said. "They don't seem to be made for humans."

"They're the new '73 models," Gigi said. "I saw pictures in this week's *Ogle*."

"I guess the fire has jammed traffic," Barnaby said. "We don't want to be stuck here if it spreads . . ." He backed, gunned forward, squeaked between two cars with a screech of metal, swerved to avoid a hurtling fire engine.

The cars ahead jammed the street solidly. A policeman blew a whistle, held up a hand as Barnaby bore down on him. He turned his back, motioned an opposing stream across the car's path.

"I've got to beat them!" Barnaby accelerated, bounced the cop aside, sent two dummy pedestrians high in the air; the on-rushing car clipped the midget car's rear bumper; Barnaby cut the wheel hard, humped up onto the sidewalk. Imitation pedestrians went down, bounced aside, spun against the aluminum walls, smiling and chatting. Barnaby shifted to second. A heap of pleased-looking dummies ground along in front of the car, piling higher. The little car's wheels spun, shifted down. The car groaned under the weight of its burden. Barnaby reversed, tried again.

"Look!" Gigi screamed. A three-foot wall of water

surged down on them from the street ahead, bearing on its crest, paper, TV sets, empty bottles, more paper . . .

The tide swirled around the sides of the car.

"All that water they're pumping—and the drains are clogged with paper!" He looked down. Playing cards, prayer books, horoscopes, racing forms, greeting cards, ticker tape, efficiency reports, tax forms . . .

"They use a lot of paper here," he said. Nixon floated past. "The free peoples . . ." he said, "the free peoples . . ."

"If the water gets much deeper, we've had it!" Barnaby called.

A swirl of smoke drifted across the street. A tongue of flame leaped high. Sparks shot skyward in a bright column as a building collapsed.

Barnaby gunned the car; it jittered forward. Water boiled up over the wheels, surged higher, seeped in under the doors.

"The upholstery is dissolving!" Gigi called over the roar of water and fire. "We'll have to get inside a building, up on an upper floor!"

"And burn alive? I'd rather drown——"

A small aluminum rowboat appeared, riding the flood.

"Catch it, Barnaby!" Gigi squealed. He flung the car door open, scrambled on the hood. As the boat whirled past, he lunged, caught the rope trailing from the bow.

"Get in, Gigi!" The girl scrambled over the thwart; Barnaby jumped, tossed overboard the sign reading BE THE NEIGHBORHOOD OUTDOOR MAN! KEEP A BOAT IN YOUR BACKYARD!

"Who's got a backyard?" Barnaby muttered, unshipping the oars. The boat whirled, steadied, shot into an alley. Barnaby plied the oars, steered around a flooded-out Dempster Dumpster.

"Barnaby, can't you row us away from the fire?" Gigi quavered. Barnaby looked over his shoulder; the current was carrying the boat directly toward a dense pall of billowing black smoke.

"It's all I can do to keep us head-on, so we don't capsize," he gasped.

"Ohhh, Barnaby, I'm scared!"

The smoke ahead was shot through with orange light now; a leaping tower of fire showed briefly at roof-top level. The current bubbled and frothed, smelling faintly of raspberry soda.

"Barnaby, maybe we'd better swim for it!"

"Stay in the boat—maybe I can maneuver it down a side street."

Sparks whirled, settling over the boat. Gigi yelped and slapped at an ember. The water was up to door-top level along the street now, a furious torrent.

"Good-bye, Barnaby!" Gigi threw herself into his lap, her arms around his neck.

"Hey, Gigi—how can I row——"

A deafening boom! blanked off the crash of the flood. The light winked from the scene; abruptly, it was night, sparkling with blazing floodlights that showed a heaving surface of dirty water clotted with flotsam, a fallen wall, the dim bulks of massive machines.

"Gigi! We're back!" Barnaby held on as the boat swept past the remnants of the control room at terrific speed, dashed for a wide, lighted doorway over which Barnaby caught a glimpse of the words GOOBER ENTERPRISES blazoned in gold. Then with a rush the boat was past the portal, sliding down a wide corridor, rocking wildly as the subsiding flood surged around a corner, curled through an open door. The keel grounded with a soggy squeak; the last of the water soaked into the deep-pile carpet. From behind a massive desk, Harlow Goober glared, his electro-lenses like tiny windows in a purple balloon. He opened his mouth and bellowed . . .

"It really wasn't my fault," Barnaby Quale said to his cellmate. "All I did was——"

"Yeah, I heard all about you, bub. Some caper. I seen the excitement on the tube. Like a kind of a bubble of force, the guy said, two blocks wide and gaining ten feet an hour. They couldn't get inside for nothing. And power for the whole state was dimmed out for three hours!"

"There must have been some malfunction," Barnaby said. "The field wasn't supposed to expand. Of course, since it was a closed-space effect, no external force could have any influence on it. But as for power, how was I to know Goober was tapping the state power pile? That's a Federal offense."

"Maybe—but with his pull, who's to care?"

There was a clank of feet from the corridor; a uniformed guard appeared at the barred door.

"Okay, you guys, on yer feet. You got a Very Important Visitor . . ."

The massive, paunched figure of Harlow Goober hove into view.

"There you are, Clune! Where you deserve to be!" He held out a hand and a small nervous man hovering at his heels placed a floral-patterned tissue in it. He mopped at his jowls. "After all Goober Industries has done for you, you turn on her and savage her! In your frenzy, you stooped to sabotage! You——"

"All I did was try out your Goobereality machine, Mr. Goober," Barnaby said flatly. "And what I saw in there——"

"Ah—we'll go into that later, Gerb; I came here this morning to offer you forgiveness. Yes, forgiveness, Creen; out of consideration of your past services——"

"You mean inventing all the things that you've made a fortune on? Think nothing of it, Mr. Goober; I enjoy my work. And after all, you were paying me union scale, and I wasn't even a member."

Goober shook his head. "Ever the lone wolf, eh, Deeb? But that's enough gossiping; I'm in a hurry." He held out a hand and the small courtier placed a document in it. Goober offered it through the bars.

"Just sign this contract, and I'll overlook your running amok——"

"I didn't run amok, Mr. Goober; I just wanted to see how my Environmental Simulator worked. Your engineers did a first-class job of building it. But the things I saw in there——"

"Shhh! Corporate secrets, Kerp! Just sign this and we can go along and have a quiet chat in my office."

"I'm not signing anything, Mr. Goober. When I tell all I know——"

"A raise, Gorp! I think you deserve it. After all, a perfect attendance record during the six years you were with us——"

"Nope. I'm going to blow the lid off. Tapping public power, eh? And——"

Goober was shaking his head pityingly. "Kipp, do you really think anyone will listen?"

"Sure." Barnaby indicated his roommate. "This fellow here already knows about it."

"Fellow," Goober said in a kindly tone, rolling an electrolens on the man, "do you know anything detrimental to the best interests of Goober Enterprises?"

"Sure, Mr. Goober! I mean, heck no, Mr. Goober! I mean, say, I'll sign anything you like, only just get me outa here——"

"You'll be sprung by nightfall, my man," Goober said grandly. "I can see there's been a miscarriage of justice."

"An abortion, you mean!" Quale shouted. "Look here, Goober——"

"All I want from you, my dear Queeb, is a full report on your findings while inside the environmental field. Decree of virisimilitude, accuracy of detail, consistency of illusion, tactile, olfactory and——"

"Go take a look for yourself!" Barnaby snapped. "I'm not one of your guinea pigs."

"In the name of science, Geep! I appeal to your sense of intellectual responsibility! You were there, a trained observer——"

"Send in your own crew, or is the thing permanently off the air?"

"The Simulator is back in readiness for use; it wasn't damaged, thank heaven! But I've had to postpone the demonstratin indefinitely."

Quale laghed sharply. "Having a little trouble getting volunteers, are you?"

"It's your fault, Queep! You scared the wits out of us—I mean out of them! That field interface was like a wall of rubbery steel! Then when it started to expand, it simply gobbled up everything it touched! Dissolved the experimental shed as though it were a cookie in hot water! Used the matter to convert into the illusion, I suppose!

"And the power drain! It was rising at the rate of

seventy-two percent per hour! And we were helpless to shut it down. You know about the automatic interlocks that operate during a power flow; the Governor suggested a fusion bomb, but our calculations revealed the Simulator would merely consume the energy and put on a spurt! If the Simulator hadn't shorted out—due to the flood, I assume—it would be growing yet! It's a Frankenstein, Geel! And it's all your fault!

"Now, the least you can do is tell me what you saw in there! What was it like? Plenty of brand names in evidence, I assume. You saw consumers in action; what were they consuming? I spent over a hundred thousand dollars programing typical audience characteristics into that panel. I have a right to know what the machine came up with!"

Barnaby sat back on his bunk, folded his arms. "Nuts to you, Goober," he said. "Figure it out for yourself."

Goober turned an unusual shade of magenta.

"I'll see you sealed in concrete five hundred feet underground, Gerp!" he grated. He whirled, collided with his toady, snarled and stalked away.

"Boy, you're nuts to rile Mr. Goober thataway," Barnaby's roomy said pityingly. "Look at me: I'm getting sprung, and by tonight I'll be putting on the feedbag with a swell doll down at Ration House Number Seventy-nine. All you hadda do was go along with the gag and you coulda been sitting pretty too."

"Nuts to Goober," Barnaby said shortly. He went to the door, fiddled with the lock. There was a click; the door swung open an inch.

"Hey!" Barnaby said. "It's not locked . . ."

"So what. Look, whyncha send word to Goober that you been thinking——"

"I can walk right out," Barnaby said. He poked his head out and looked along the corridor.

"Are you nuts? What's out there? Without you got a job, you're better off right here. You get three squares, plenty TV, lotsa sob-sisters sending in bound volumes of Playboy and the National Geographic. You got security here, man! Don't knock it!"

157

"I've got an idea," Barnaby said. "In fact, I've got a couple of ideas. Listen, friend, if they ask, just tell them you didn't notice me leaving. Say you were asleep. You can do that much for a fellow jailbird, can't you?"

"I think yer cookie's crumbled, pal, but if that's the way you want it, okay."

"Thanks. Arrividerci!" Barnaby slipped through the door and moved off toward the light at the far end.

"Barnaby!" Gigi squeaked. "Where did you——"

"Shhh! Don't attract any attention." Quale eased through the door into the girl's six by eight cubicle. "I'm glad you were here, Gigi. I was afraid you'd be in jail too."

"In jail! Oh, Barnaby, is that where——"

"Yep. Goober tried to buy me off, but I didn't go for it. For a while I had ideas about exposing Goober's racket, but a legal expert I ran into pointed out the impracticality of that."

"But, Barnaby—if you don't go to work for Mr. Goober——"

"And give up the last shred of hope for independence? I'd rather starve!"

"But what can we do?"

Barnaby took her hand. "You did say 'we'?"

"Of course, Barnaby Quale. You're insane, but I love you . . . and I guess it's because you *are* insane—wanting to do things your own way, when the Government's got a program for everything already taped."

"I hoped you'd feel that way. We'll lie low till dark and then make our move. Listen, here's what I have in mind . . ."

It was dark in the Experimental Complex, except for the floodlit circles where workmen still toiled to clear away the last of the ring of debris left by the flash flood from the abruptly terminated simulated environment. Barnaby and Gigi rounded the end of the Admin Building, surveyed the site of last night's holocaust. Where the big shed had been, only the massive shapes of the equipment housings squatted against bare ground.

"You see? The field got out of hand," Barnaby breathed. "It developed some kind of self-perpetuating feedback; started cannibalizing everything around, and building itself bigger. Naturally, the apparatus itself was exempt because it was isolated from the field by the way the antennas were strung. And it had the whole state's power supply to draw on. And come to think of it, with the emergency interlock system, it can tap the whole supply for North America—and probably South America too."

"Barnaby, what if somebody catches us? After last night——"

"We won't think about that. Let's go." Keeping the shadows, he approached the tarp-covered control console. While Gigi watched nervously for patrolling guards, Barnaby cut through tie-down ropes, lifted the Gooberplast cover, slipped under it.

"Barnaby, hurry!" Gigi hissed.

"Sure, it will only take a few minutes . . ." He switched on a small flashlight, propped it by the panel.

"Now, let's see," he muttered. "First I'll have to code in some instructions about interactions between the environment and the external observers, namely Gigi and myself . . ."

The tarp twitched. "Barnaby! They see us! There's a spotlight!"

"Hold on just a minute longer!" Quale called. "I'm almost done!" He punched keys, wiping sweat from his brow with the back of his hand. ". . . weather . . . crops . . . architecture . . . vegetation . . ."

A siren wailed. Barnaby heard a hoarse voice shout. Gigi squeaked. He scrambled from under the tarp, took her hand. "Okay, if everything works, we're ready . . ." He jumped to the large lever, hauled it down. The humming noise started up. There were clicks and rumbles from underground. The big red light on the panel blinked on. Barnaby reached, punched the ACTIVATE button. The humming deepened. A dim light sprang up; something seemed to shimmer at the center of the bare expanse of concrete . . .

"Get ready!" Barnaby took Gigi's hand.

There was a dull boom! and the air whistled furiously

past Barnaby's head. A curtain of gray fog hung before him. He swallowed hard, took a step, felt a tingle as the mist parted before him . . .

Bright sunlight gleamed on a grassy field where immense wildflowers nodded to a gentle breeze. Woods clothed the nearby hills, and on the crest of a low mountain a castle stood, pennants fluttering from its towers. An odor of spring filled the air.

"Barnaby, it's lovely!" Gigi breathed. "Do you really think we're safe here?"

"Certainly. It is nice, isn't it? I had to work pretty fast, but I think I got it all in."

"Barnaby! I just happened to think! What about the people? Will it just . . . convert them too?"

"They'll be screened and modified to fit the specs. After all, they're part of the environment, too."

There was a sound behind them; they turned. A vast man in a blue jacket and knee breeches was standing looking about with a perplexed smile. He saw Barnaby and the girl and doffed his pointed hat with a jingle of bells.

"Greetings, friends," he called.

"Why, it's Mr. Goober!" Gigi gasped.

Barnaby nodded approvingly. "If it handled Goober, we're in," he said. "Come on, let's explore."

"Why, look," Gigi said, "it's a paved road . . ."

"Of course," Barnaby nodded approvingly.

Gigi looked back. "Shouldn't we take Mr. Goober with us? He's just sitting there, smelling the flowers."

"He'll be all right," Barnaby said. "This is his chance to make new friends." He took Gigi's hand and together they started off along the yellow brick road.